# RENOVATING LOVE

# RENOVATING LOVE

•

## Mary Leask

**AVALON BOOKS**
NEW YORK

PRINTED IN THE UNITED STATES OF AMERICA
ON ACID-FREE PAPER
BY HADDON CRAFTSMEN, BLOOMSBURG, PENNSYLVANIA

This book is dedicated to Dr. Joaquin Kuhn and his
writing group, to Karen Hogg; friend, writer and valuable critic
and to Bob Mason whose childhood home was the inspiration
for this novel.

*Chapter One*

Pushing himself away from his computer, David stretched his arms and ran his fingers through a mass of sandy curls; curls that in the past he had kept closely cropped but were now allowed to riot about his head. Standing, he turned off his computer. There, he thought, that's the end of it. Project finished. Now I can get on with my new life and the first order of business is this house. The second order of business, he frowned and then shrugged—I'll just have to resolve that problem later.

David looked about the room critically. It was in terrible shape. Ancient beige wallpaper hung in limp strips revealing cracked plaster and, here and there, the lath beneath. The tall double-hung windows had lost their varnish and in several places the putty was missing. The wooden frames were rotting.

His friends thought he was crazy to buy an old house out in the middle of nowhere, but it turned out to be exactly what he needed. He'd proven that by finishing a project in two months that normally would have taken four.

He liked the quiet of the old house, even though he had to ignore the scurry of rodent feet and the sighs of the wind through various cracks in door and window frames. The house was free of the frenetic sound of humans at work. There were no machines running except his computer, no interruptions and no bad air. Even better, there were no management decisions to make and no employees to deal with. As far as he was concerned, it was heaven, even if the odd angel had whiskers and a tail.

However, on this wonderfully warm spring day when the air outside was full of bird song and a dusting of green buds tinted the trees, he knew he would have to adjust to unfamiliar noises if he wanted to spend the following winter in the house. It was time to renovate.

He'd asked numerous people in the nearby village of Stewart's Falls to recommend the best renovating company and, without exception, the answer was Thompson Builders and Renovators. Picking up the phone, he dialed their number. In short order, he arranged for a member of the company to come over the next day.

Feeling quite pleased with himself, David walked into the kitchen. If the living room was in poor shape, the kitchen was even worse: a stained enamel sink was set in a badly discolored counter, dark linoleum with numerous cracks covered the floor, and a single light hung from the ceiling. Originally, anything above a sixty-watt bulb blew the circuits. Before he was able to use his computer or the heaters that he needed for warmth, it had been necessary to have a new electrical service installed and the wiring updated in the kitchen and living room. The rest could be done once the renovators started work.

But David loved the old kitchen anyway. It shared one wing of the T-shaped house with two small rooms which had probably been small bedrooms originally. The kitchen had two exits; one led to a verandah running the length of the wing, the other was tucked in at the back where the two wings intersected.

The old kitchen was very large; large enough he hoped to accommodate a modern kitchen and family room. Maybe a fireplace could be added in the space as well. He puzzled over the idea for a moment, trying to visualize it. With a shrug, he decided the renovators would know how to plan such an arrangement.

Jim Thompson returned the phone to its cradle. Well, well, he thought. The old McIsaac place. Imagine someone wanting to renovate that house.

Just then, he heard a vehicle drive up. Going to the window, he saw his daughter Carolyn step out of the company van. As always, he felt a surge of affection for her. Without her willingness to help over the past four years, the company probably would have failed. After his heart attack, she dropped out of her architectural course and took over the running of the business as well as working on her specialty, carpentry and cabinetmaking.

She was the only one of his offspring who had the breadth of experience to oversee the business, although the rest of his children excelled in their own areas. Ben oversaw the plumbing, Andy was an electrician and Mike, the oldest, ran the heavy machinery and was expert in building foundations as well as moving and lifting structures.

He smiled a welcome when Carolyn entered and walked across to his desk. With a flourish, she handed him a check and a copy of an invoice. "There you are, Dad. Paid in full. The end of the Hepburn project."

He watched his daughter as she put the rest of her materials on her desk. He still found it amusing that the smallest member of his very tall family should be the one who most suitably fit into his shoes. Even then, her shortness was only by comparison to his other children.

She stood five feet, nine inches tall. A swathe of long, dark hair tied back with a pink ribbon rippled down her back. Sparkling blue eyes conveyed her pleasure at the finished business. In his opinion, it didn't matter how she was dressed, she always looked feminine. Today, she wore jeans on her long slim legs and a soft green and blue cotton, plaid shirt over a blue T-shirt. Tiny pearl studs were visible on her ears.

He indicated a chair near his desk. "Take a seat, honey. I've got some exciting news for you."

Her eyes lit up as she guessed. "A new project? Great."

He couldn't help grinning with pleasure as he said, "You remember the old McIsaac place?"

"You're kidding." When he indicated he was serious, she jumped up, unable to contain her excitement. "The old McIsaac place. Wow! I've wanted to get my hands on that house for years. It has such fantastic potential and the location is so beautiful."

She went to her desk and grabbed a writing pad. "Okay. Tell me the particulars." Even as she spoke, she was sketching the front view of the house from memory.

It was typical of the two-storied farmhouses built in the area at the end of the nineteenth century. Often they looked as if two houses were stuck together to form a

"T" or an "L." Each face had a gable over an arched window on the second floor. At least one side had a verandah across its front.

Carolyn loved old farmhouses like this one. They dotted the countryside between Stewart's Falls and Toronto. Often, they could be perched on a hill or located down a long country lane. And almost always, the gable edges were decorated with inventive gingerbread carvings painted white. She decorated the gable in her drawing with an elegantly scrolled trim.

"Hey," her father cautioned. "Don't get too carried away. So far, all we have is an invitation to send someone out to discuss the project with the owner. His name is David Reid. Ever heard of him?"

She frowned. "No. In fact, I haven't been out that way in over a year. I wasn't aware anyone had bought the place."

"Well, you have an appointment with him tomorrow at ten o'clock. He said we were the company recommended most frequently. It sounds as if the job is ours if we can meet his needs. So do your best."

Carolyn leaned over and kissed his forehead. "Always, Dad."

He patted her arm. "I know, dear."

David turned off the vacuum cleaner. He was amused with himself for feeling he had to clean the two rooms he used before letting in the contractor. It was a total waste of time. The more he vacuumed, the more dust seemed to appear. As he picked up the machine and stuck it under the cot that sat in the corner of the kitchen, a movement outside caught his eye. Walking to the window, he saw a silver van come to a stop in the driveway.

The words *Thompson Builders and Renovators* were tastefully stenciled on the side.

As he watched, a young woman stepped out of the van. She wore a white cotton shirt under a light blue jacket, blue jeans and heavy workboots. Under one arm she carried a clipboard, and in her hand a hard hat. David groaned. A woman! He didn't want to deal with a woman, and especially not one who wore workboots. In his experience, such women were always opinionated, bossy, and poor listeners and he had no desire to spend his time being told what he wanted.

David listened for two people's steps on the verandah but heard only one set. Scowling, he headed for the old screen door.

Carolyn could not suppress her pleasure as she admired what had been the most formal of the house's three entrances. The doorway was quite elegant, with glass transom and sidelights. She couldn't help but notice an old, discolored brass chime on the door. With a little hard work, she thought, it would shine as good as new.

She continued around the house to an entrance under a long verandah. She knew from experience that this would lead to the original kitchen and was the entrance used daily by the family back at the turn of the century. After climbing the stairs and crossing the verandah, she knocked on the old-fashioned screen door and waited.

Behind the screen the figure of a very tall man appeared. She was surprised. He looked much younger than she'd expected, no more than thirty or thirty-two. He stood with his hands on his hips, inspecting her. She returned him look for look. He was at least five inches taller than she. A mass of sandy hair curled around his long narrow face. He wasn't handsome, yet he had presence. His grey eyes suggested intelligence and something else.

Suddenly it dawned on her that the owner of those eyes was irritated, looking down his nose with impatience, waiting for her to say something. She pulled a business card from her shirt pocket and said, "Hi. I'm Carolyn Thompson. I'm from Thompson Builders and Renovators. I believe you were expecting me."

She stopped talking when she realized he was looking out over her head through the screen as if expecting someone else. She looked behind her but could see no one. Looking back at the man she asked, "You are David Reid, aren't you?"

He was frowning now. "Where is Mr. Thompson? I had an appointment with him."

"I'm afraid my father does the planning in the office these days, Mr. Reid. My three brothers and I do the legwork."

He made no reply but instead, opened the door and indicated she should enter, forcing her to squeeze past his rather intimidating height. Abruptly, he turned and walked through the kitchen and a hall to the living room. She shrugged and followed. She found his behavior bordering on rude, but couldn't afford to take offense.

Briefly, she noticed the drooping wallpaper and cracked plaster as he led her toward a desk on which sat a computer, fax machine, and telephone. A printer sat on an old wooden crate.

David Reid, for she assumed that was who he was, indicated a worn kitchen chair across from another equally disreputable one with a cushion on it. "Please have a seat. I'll go over what I would like done and we'll see if you think your company can do it." Still frowning his displeasure, he added, "I had hoped to deal with someone with more experience."

She bit her lip to keep from advising him that she'd been underfoot in the business since she was old enough to follow her father and brothers about.

Instead, she took a steadying breath and looked right into his grey eyes. "You're welcome to telephone Mr. and Mrs. Gary Hepburn. We've just finished renovating their nineteenth-century house over at Stewart's Falls under my supervision. They'll assure you that I am competent at my job. My father would not consider sending me otherwise."

Writing down a telephone number, she tore off the sheet of paper from her pad and handed it to him. "I suggest you contact them right now and check my credentials. I'll wait outside."

With that, she stood up and walked out of the room, her head held high, her long braid of hair switching back and forth like the tail of an aggravated cat.

Damn, he thought and hurried after her. As she stepped onto the verandah, letting the screen door slam, he called, "Don't you want this job?"

She turned and considered him where he stood looking out through the screen. "Of course, I want this job. I have always thought this house was far too wonderful to neglect. However, I'm not prepared to spend the entire time defending myself. Please telephone the Hepburns. If you're not satisfied with their response, then I'll leave and let you find another contractor."

He hated it when a woman backed him into a corner and that was exactly where he was at the moment. The Hepburns had been the people who had praised Thompson Builders so highly. He had even been shown through the house by the enthusiastic couple. However, he hadn't gotten where he was without learning when to change his strategy.

Pushing through the screen door, he walked over to two well-worn Adirondack chairs, angled one toward the other and admitted, "I don't need to telephone the Hepburns. I've already spoken to them. Actually, I've even seen their house. Your company did an excellent job." Gesturing to the chair, he coaxed, "Please sit down and let me tell you what I want."

Eyeing him suspiciously, she sat down but her posture suggested anything but submission. She sat straight in the slope-backed chair, her long legs bent to one side. Briskly, she pulled a pen off her clipboard and waited.

David was thrown by this action. He'd expected her to start telling him how he should renovate the house. After all, she'd said the house was too beautiful to tear down. That suggested that she already had a plan.

Sitting back, he crossed his arms over his chest and half closed his eyes. "I want this to be a house that will suit a family, a place that will encourage family togetherness. I'd like the kitchen to include a family area as well as an eating and cooking area. The kitchen should be a place where a man or woman would enjoy cooking. If possible, I'd like a fireplace somewhere in the family room."

He paused for a moment and glanced over at her. When she realized he was watching her, she hurriedly made a note of what he'd said, then waited.

Surprised that she was not interrupting, he continued. "I'd like the main hall to be restored to its original beauty, if possible. I think the front door can be saved. If not, I'd like it to be replicated. The same for the staircase and the window at the top of the stairs."

He waited until she finished writing and then suggested, "It might be wise if you were to examine the house now, and then we can discuss the other rooms. I haven't as many opinions about them."

As they stood up, she did something that completely floored him. In spite of the antagonism that had flared between them mere minutes ago, she smiled, a look of genuine pleasure in her lovely blue eyes. "I appreciate it when a client knows what he or she wants. It makes the task so much easier."

With that, she turned and went down the steps. He watched her as she disappeared around the side of the house. She confused him. She wasn't what he'd expected of a woman who wore wookboots and a hard hat.

Minutes later, she reappeared on the other side and began another circuit, this time examining the stone foundation, poking at the spaces between the stones; the highways, he believed, of his resident rodents.

He returned to his computer to tidy up the accumulation of papers from his finished project, but only part of his mind was on his work. The other part was listening to her footsteps as she walked through the rooms, up into the attic and down into the basement.

Carolyn breathed a sigh of relief when he'd finally gone back into the house. They needed this job and she'd almost ruined everything by losing her temper. But he'd been so arrogant. She couldn't hide a smug little smile when she recalled his admission that he knew their work was good.

She worked steadily for an hour and a half. First she examined the very worn foundation, then proceeded to check the peach-colored brick exterior. She was pleasantly surprised to discover that the brickwork had recently been repaired. She prowled around in the cool, mouse-infested basement and climbed up to the bat-filled attic. She even climbed a rather weary television tower and checked the roof.

When she finished making her notes about these areas, she went inside and headed for the second floor. Climbing up the once elegant stairs, she was surprised to come face-to-face with an arched stained glass window. Normally, she would have expected the window to be made of ordinary glass. A narrow hall ran along three sides of the stairwell leading into a series of bedrooms, large and small. Glancing into them, Carolyn's imagination was immediately set into motion. The possibilities for renovation were endless.

She returned downstairs and stood in the kitchen. This area was going to be a challenge. It was large and boxy with two small rooms situated on the outside wall. There were long windows on the front and rear. It would take imagination to combine the kitchen and family area he wanted. One of the small rooms could be useful as a laundry and mudroom. She'd have to think about the other.

She went out into the hall and entered what must have been the dining room. It was full of boxes but she was able to move them just enough to check the wood-paneled walls. She ran her hand over the dusty surface. There was surprisingly little damage. She was sure that it could be restored, and what a magnificent room it would be.

It was while she was pushing back some boxes containing pictures that one in particular caught her eye. It wasn't a picture but rather a diploma bearing David Reid's name. A doctorate—in mathematics and computer engineering. She hadn't realized one could do both at the same time. She looked at the date and realized that the degree had been earned some years ago when David was in his early twenties. She whistled to herself. He had to be extremely clever. Well, that explains it, she thought. He's true to form. I should have recognized the type. I've had enough experience to distinguish brainy, autocratic, arrogant, sarcastic men when I meet them.

Carolyn stood quietly looking out the window. The house was built on a hilly peninsula with a spectacular view of a lake on three sides. The view, however, was lost to her at the moment. Instead, she was recalling James; James who had captivated her when she first entered the university.

James was tall, handsome, and intellectually stimulating—especially for a young woman who was living on her own for the first time. Initially, he had enchanted her with his charm and sophisticated behavior. As time passed, he quietly began to belittle her while attempting to change her. Finally, when she had most needed support, he was nowhere to be found. She'd vowed then that she would avoid the pedantic crowd for the rest of her life.

Now she knew why David Reid aggravated her. Although he didn't speak in the cultivated manner that James had perfected, he had certainly been prepared to belittle her in the same way. Well, let him try. He would find that she was up to the challenge. She was no longer the pushover she'd been as a young university student from a small town.

She returned to the living room where David was packing materials into a box. She studied him for a moment. For such a tall man, he moved with an economy of motion. Her awareness of his height annoyed her. Being a tall woman herself, she knew that such a man always evoked her interest. Was she genetically programed to notice every six-footer she encountered? she wondered. Regardless, she didn't like her prickling of interest. She worked with men all the time, enjoyed their company and got along with them quite well. This situation should be no different.

Deliberately she focused her attention on the living room. Just about everything in this area needed work. Mentally, she calculated an estimate of the cost to repair it and added it to the other figures she'd noted on her clipboard. Totaling them, she whistled silently. This job was going to cost considerably more than the Hepburn's.

Suddenly, he sensed her presence and turned. "Well, Ms. Thompson, have you seen enough?" Although the question was innocuous enough, she sensed antagonism when he spoke. Why? she wondered. What was it about her that bothered him?

"I've had a good look around the place. If you have a few minutes, there are some questions I'd like to ask."

He frowned at this. "You're the expert, Ms. Thompson. I assume you can make the decisions without me assisting you."

"And you are the customer, Mr. Reid. I am certain you'd like a voice when there is a decision to be made that affects your comfort or your pocketbook."

She waited. She could see that he didn't like her reply nor did he like dealing with her. Well, tough. Her dad was not well enough to be dragging himself out here and none of her brothers could do the job.

Finally, he suggested, "Let's sit down on the porch." He began to lead the way, then as an afterthought, paused and asked, "Would you like a glass of lemonade?" Surprised, she nodded, then looked at her hands. "If you don't mind, I'll just freshen up."

When she returned to the porch, he was sitting in one

of the chairs, a notebook and pencil in hand, and a pitcher and glasses of lemonade ready for them on a small table. Determined to establish a better atmosphere between them, she smiled, sat down and thanked him for the lemonade.

She took a few moments to enjoy the cool drink while viewing the meadowlands, trees and lake, all the time aware that he was watching her out of the corner of his eye. When she finished the lemonade, she turned to him and began to fill him in on her general impressions.

"I have never been in this house before. I have to admit I find it very interesting."

He raised his eyebrows at this, but said nothing.

Carolyn thought for a moment, then tried to explain. "To begin with, the house is much larger than I thought. Because it has the shape of a late nineteenth-century farmhouse, I assumed it would be smaller. The extra space makes it all the more advantageous. You really chose a gem when you bought this place."

David heard her enthusiasm and yet found himself still trying to judge if she was just buttering him up, rather than genuinely meaning what she said. But he could find nothing to suggest anything but enthusiasm. Her eyes, an amazing shade of blue, sparkled as she continued to describe some of the house's potential. "The second floor has ample room to add modern bathrooms while allowing you all the bedrooms needed for a good-sized family."

Finally, she looked him straight in the eye and said, "I guess what I'm trying to say is that you can fulfill all your dreams in this house, but it will cost a great deal of money. I can't give you an exact figure yet, but I do know that you could probably build a new home meeting your requirements for a great deal less."

"I don't want a new home," David stressed. "I want this house with all its flaws renovated."

Carolyn nodded. "I just wanted to be sure you knew what you were biting off before we began."

David stood and looked out over the verandah railing, gathering his thoughts. Turning to her, he said, "Let me make one thing clear. If we can work together. . . . If we can agree on what has to be done and if your suggestions are reasonable, then cost is not an issue. I am quite prepared to spend whatever it takes to bring this house back to its former beauty as well as modernizing the basic services. I want it to be a warm and welcoming home."

She studied him for a moment, noting the grey eyes that watched her intently, gauging her reaction to his statement. He was quite serious. The practical side of her gave a little cheer. Here was a project that would keep them all busy and well-fed for some time to come. Standing, she suggested, "Let's start with the basics. Walk around the house with me and I'll point out some of the work that must be done."

As they headed outside, she said, "Do you know why the previous owner had the brickwork repaired?"

"I forgot to tell you. He had rather grandiose plans for a bed-and-breakfast. By the time he had the brickwork completely repaired and a large septic system installed, he ran out of money."

For the next hour, they walked outside the house and then through the interior, from basement to attic. She drew his attention to the condition of the foundation, the poor wiring except where he had the new panel installed, the faulty plumbing, and the need for a new roof. To all this bad news, he just nodded. It wasn't until they came to the dining room, with its rich wood paneling, that they ran into difficulty.

She entered the room ahead of him and ran her hand across the wood. "This will be the most beautiful room in your house when it's restored. The paneling is quite wonderful. It will be a glorious room in which to entertain your guests at dinner."

She glanced at him only to encounter a frown of annoyance. "Hold it, Ms. Thompson. This is not going to be the dining room. I plan to have this room for a study. The view from these windows is superb. I like to be able to look out while I'm thinking. I know exactly how I want this study to be."

It was all she could do not to argue with him. But she realized that she would never win. It was his house. And she had learned that it was well to hear the owner out, to listen to his or her ideas, then to try to solve the aesthetic problems later.

When she did not disagree with him, he felt he had to explain further. "I told you that I wanted this house designed for a family. This room is the farthest from the family room. I can work quietly here without being disturbed by the children."

For some reason, she had thought he was unmarried. He wore no wedding ring and there was no sign of a wife and children. She couldn't resist asking, "How many children do you have, Mr. Reid?"

She was fascinated at his change of expression. He actually blushed. "Uhmm." He seemed to search for words. "Actually, I don't have any yet."

Interested, and for some reason, unable to let it go, she asked, "Shouldn't your wife be involved with the decisions on these renovations?"

This time, he looked downright uncomfortable. "I'm not married." He paused and then added, "Yet."

She would think later that she really had been dumb. She'd missed the whole point of his embarrassment. Instead, she soldiered on with her questions. "Well, wouldn't your fiancée want to be part of this process?"

With that, he exploded. "Ms. Thompson. For your information, I do not have a fiancée, nor do I have a wife. I am the one making the decisions." Then, he headed for the door. Pausing for a moment, he added, "But I intend to have a wife. I expect the house to be ready by the time I've chosen one."

For a moment, Carolyn was stunned by these last statements. Then, as he disappeared out of sight, she had to bite her lip to keep from laughing. He was preparing a house for a wife he'd not even selected? She shook her head. Such confidence. Checking her notes, Carolyn determined she had all the information required to work out what was needed to make the house a "warm and welcoming home."

Taking her leave of David Reid, she walked about the property one last time. A large wooden cabin stood farther back on the lot that she wanted to inspect. She had a notion about this building.

It was made of weathered board-and-batten pine. The interior was large and constructed with solid beams. Checking outside, she saw that it was placed on cement blocks. From the look of it, it had been placed there recently. Even more informative was the newer boarding at one end of the cabin.

She made a note of the building's size. It was really quite large. The more she looked at the structure, the more she liked its lines. Walking back to the house, she carefully examined the ground around it. Just as she suspected, the structure had originally been an addition to the house; probably as a summer kitchen. There were traces of the foundation behind the kitchen wing.

As she drove home, she couldn't help a shiver of excitement. She always felt that way when starting a new job.

## *Chapter Two*

Davidd sat by the restaurant window, sipping his coffee
and enjoying the view of the park opposite the café. The
evening sun shone through the willows that lined the
river meandering through the park, casting shadows over
the water and across the rich green lawn. Children played
on a set of swings while parents sat at a picnic table
gossiping. A group of pigeons twirled before an old man
as he tossed bread crumbs to them.

David ate at this café frequently. The food, though
simple, was good. Because the specialty of the house was
fish and chips, a cross-section of the population of Stewart's Falls came in during the week. Over time, he'd
begun to make friends with the other people who were
regular customers.

The sound of a child's serious voice at a table nearby
caught David's attention. A young couple sat eating with
their two boys, approximately six and eight years old.

They were well-behaved youngsters, busy nibbling on their chips and chatting with their parents.

A warm feeling of anticipation flooded through David. This was his dream; children of his own, eating out as a family, playing in the park across the road, walking down the road to the school beyond the park.

He'd worked so very hard, driven by a talent that wouldn't let him rest. But now, he had more success than any man needed, more wealth than he could ever use. From now on he intended to spend his energy on activities that would broaden his knowledge and, hopefully, be useful to others. Even more importantly, he would spend time with his wife and children. He'd grown up in a close family and had missed the richness of family life when he'd been so focused on his work. He wanted to regain that richness now.

The children reminded him of his conversation with Carolyn Thompson. He'd had no intention of telling her that he didn't have a wife or even a fiancée but somehow, she'd dug away at him and he'd had to confess the truth. He could just imagine the laugh she'd had at his expense. Even he knew it was preposterous to think one could simply find a partner in the same efficient fashion one selected a new car or house. Still, he believed that when one's mind was open to new influences, they, just like ideas, could develop into something quite different and exciting.

Leaning back in his chair, he glanced out the window again. The movement of people at the end of the park caught his eye. He realized they must be playing on the tennis courts which had finally opened.

That reminded him of something. He pulled a folded newspaper from his pocket. It was a small edition titled *The Stewart's Falls Gazette*. He'd already glanced at it but now he turned to the last inside page and found what he was looking for, an advertisement for new members at the tennis club. It seemed the community organization was available to anyone willing to pay a small fee. Nodding to himself, he left money on the table to cover his bill and tip and headed off in the direction of the players.

David approached the tennis courts casually, drifting to the fence and watching where three sets of doubles played. Standing around watching the players was a group of people of all ages dressed for tennis and waiting their turn. Studying the people of his age carefully, he was pleased to see two very attractive young women cheering on the players. One of them caught his eye. She was petite, with short blond hair and nice legs. His interest was piqued. He liked short, feminine women. Then, to his disgust, his long-legged contractor's image crossed his mind. He could still see those heavy boots and that clipboard. Give him the small and dainty anytime!

The Thompsons lived about five miles from David's house and two blocks away from where the river plunged over a precipice creating a fifteen foot waterfall into a lake below. From Carolyn's bedroom window, she could hear the falls at night.

The residence was a sprawling, Victorian house with several gables and a rounded tower. Like many such homes of the period, an additional section had been added on the back. It was here that the offices of the family business were housed.

The minute supper was over, Carolyn headed to her computer, her mind already full of problems to solve and ideas to scrutinize. The first thing she did was to draft out a plan of David's house to scale according to her measurements.

Just as she finished it and printed a copy, her father came in and looked over her shoulder. After studying the blueprint for a few minutes, he whistled softly with surprise. "It's not exactly what I expected. I thought the rooms would be smaller. What's this you've sketched in with the dotted lines right behind the kitchen?"

"I found the traces of a foundation for a summer kitchen. I think that at one time there was an entrance into it from the kitchen. I am almost positive that the cabin standing at the back of the lot is the missing building. It must have been moved by one of the previous owners."

Her father nodded his agreement. Drawing up a chair, he sat down. "Well, what do you think? Can we do the job? And what about David Reid? Is he someone you can work with?"

Carolyn could not suppress the enthusiasm she felt in her answer. "I know we can do the job. It's an interesting challenge. But before I can really estimate the costs, I want to do a little research. I think I'll go over to the library and the newspaper tomorrow and check their records. I'd like to find out about the history of the building. I have a feeling that the main structure is not necessarily the original building. Parts of the foundation are much older than the construction in the house."

"And David Reid? What's he like?" inquired her father.

Carolyn frowned. "You know, I'm not quite sure. I feel he doesn't like me. I seem to irritate him for some reason."

Her father smiled. "You didn't tell him very nicely where to go at some point?"

Carolyn couldn't hide the guilty expression that crossed her face. "Actually, he was rather arrogant. He implied that I was not up to the job. He expected a man." She paused for a moment while her father waited, an expression of intense interest on his face. He knew such an attitude would rub his daughter the wrong way.

When she didn't continue, he coached, "And?"

With a sigh, she confessed. "I told him to telephone the Hepburns and after speaking with them, to get in touch with me if he was still interested. Then I headed for the door."

"Ca-ro-line! Temper, temper," he teased.

"Well, it cooled him down. He had to backpedal immediately. He admitted that he had not only met the Hepburns, but also been taken through their home. Then, he rather ungraciously agreed to let me work.

"Of course, nothing is settled. I am going to work out a few basic ideas to accommodate his needs and also do some research on the history of the house. When I'm ready, I'll show him what I've got and see exactly what he likes and what needs to be changed. After that, I can start to price the job."

Curious, Jim asked, "What are his special needs?"

"Well, he wants to make a warm and loving home."

Jim was impressed. "How many members in his family?"

Carolyn couldn't help but chuckle. "None. No wife, no fiancée, and no children."

Her father looked confused. "But . . ."

Carolyn tried to keep a straight face as she said, "He intends to have a wife by the time we finish the house." Then, she had to grin, "But I gather he hasn't selected the lady in question yet."

Her father's face was a study. He was definitely trying

to get his mind around this piece of rather juicy gossip. Then, the devil twinkled in his eyes as he said, "I guess that's a piece of information we should keep to ourselves." He couldn't resist adding, "Well, maybe he'll choose you."

Carolyn got up, turned off her work lamp and headed out of the office. "In your dreams, father dear."

Three days later, Carolyn drove to David's, ready to share her ideas and research with him. When she got out of the van, she was surprised to see him out behind the house digging up the remains of what must have been a kitchen garden. When he made no effort to stop, she walked over to him.

As she approached, he called, "I'll be with you in a moment. I just want to finish this row, then I'm done."

For early May, it was hot and David wore only a pair of beige work shorts and beat-up duck boots. A bright red handkerchief twisted around his forehead kept his untidy mass of curls away from his face. Carolyn could not help but notice that in spite of the fact that he must spend a lot of time at the computer, he was in very good shape. With each thrust of the shovel, the muscles in his back and arms flexed. Sunlight danced on the fine sheen of perspiration that covered his skin.

Suddenly, sanity returned. *I must be crazy*, she thought. *James was a great-looking guy and look where that got me.* Deciding that it was silly to stand there gaping at all that male muscle, she said, "I'll wait for you on the verandah, Dr. Reid."

He turned at that, demanding, "How do you know about the doctor bit?"

Somewhat taken back by his obvious annoyance, Carolyn found herself stammering, "I . . . err . . . saw your diploma when I was inspecting the dining room. I wasn't trying to pry."

As he turned to dig the shovel into the hard ground again, he said, "Well, I wish you'd forget you saw it. Too many people start treating you as if you're some kind of oddity. David will do."

Without another word, he continued his digging.

As Carolyn walked back to the verandah, she couldn't help but recall that James had insisted that everyone know he had a doctorate. On the verandah, she found a small table in a corner and brought it over to the two chairs, then set out her materials.

A short while later, her client appeared already showered and to her relief, wearing a white cotton shirt and shorts. Even then, his long legs and bare feet were a distraction.

He'd brought another tall pitcher of lemonade and glasses which he placed on the table between them. He went back into the house and returned with a notebook and a pencil. Pouring a glass of lemonade, he handed it to her and then poured himself one and settled in the chair.

She waited, rather fascinated as he emptied an entire glass. This time, his grin was disarming. "It's hot work out there in the garden." Then after a pause, "I can't wait until the house is finished and I can start working on the grounds seriously."

"You sound as if you know quite a bit about gardening," Carolyn observed.

"I should," he said. "I grew up working in a nursery. My family own Reid's Nurseries in Whitby. My father and brother are masters of horticulture."

Carolyn could not resist asking, "How come you didn't follow in their footsteps?"

David shrugged. "I guess my brain is wired differently. I just fell in love with math and its use in computers. I don't regret not going into the family business. I do enjoy gardening immensely as a hobby though. I have great plans for this yard."

Carolyn was impressed. He seemed quite content with this hobby that involved skills so different from his specialty. James, by contrast, had no use for anything that required physical labor.

Finishing another glass of lemonade, David turned to her and said, "Okay, what have you got for me."

As she pulled a sheaf of papers from her case, Carolyn asked, "Do you know much about the history of this house?"

David shook his head. "I just liked the location, thought the house had potential and bought it. At the time, I was really busy at work, so I didn't have a chance to investigate further."

"Well, I did a little research."

David raised his eyebrows at that. He hadn't figured she'd be the type to do research. He'd always found that bossy women tended to make up their minds about things without asking too many questions. At least, that had been his unfortunate experience.

Carolyn continued. "I was fairly certain that this house was not the original one on this site. The foundation is intriguing. There is an inner foundation and then a larger one around it as if the second builder couldn't be bothered removing the first. For that matter, the old one helped since this a very large house. Both foundations were made of fieldstone which explains why you have the local wildlife in residence. Quite frankly, I wonder how you keep the mice away from your computer."

"You haven't met Charlie."

"Charlie?" she queried.

David's eyes suddenly focused beyond her head. "And speak of the devil, here he is. The scourge of the mouse population with a gift for me."

Carolyn followed his glance and discovered a rather comical cat approaching with a mouse hanging from his mouth. The cat was black and white. The shape of a black handlebar mustache through his white muzzle gave him an oddly formal appearance. This was enhanced by a very white shirt. It was quite clear that the cat was a most proficient hunter because the mouse had obviously been killed swiftly and neatly. With a series of trills, the cat presented David with the mouse by putting it tidily on the floor before him. Then, he hopped up on David's shoulder and rubbed his face against David's jaw.

David scratched the cat's ears and murmured, "Good boy," then took a small container of cat treats out of the pocket of his shorts and rewarded him. Smiling at Carolyn, he explained, "I have to keep my mouser happy." Leaning forward, he picked up the mouse by the tail and threw it out over the verandah railing into a distant group of bushes. "The raccoon's supper," he explained. "It'll keep those rascals away from my bird feeders."

For a moment, David stroked the cat's fur fondly, then, as if remembering where he was and who he was with, he tipped the cat onto the verandah floor and asked, "Uhmm, what did you discover that explained the foundation?"

His question brought Carolyn back to her research. She explained. "Angus Stewart established the sawmill in town in the 1840s. Achieving some success, he built a small wooden house for his family just outside of town on this same road. Do you remember noticing the remains of a boarded-up old house just before the Henry's farm?"

David nodded.

"That was Angus's first house. However, he became so successful that in 1860 he built a larger house. You can see the remains of the old foundation under this house. Members of the family continued to live here until hard times forced them to sell.

"Robert McIsaac bought the house in 1885. In 1890, the house burnt down. He had the present house built on the same site and incorporated the old foundation. McIsaac must have had a great deal of fun planning this house."

"How so?"

"Well, he improvised. He kept the traditional plan but made it much larger. He had a variety of verge boards trim the gables." David frowned at her description, so she explained further. "It's an architectural term for gingerbread trim. And you'll notice touches of pretension. The stained glass window at the top of the stairs, the sidelights and transom around the main door and the wonderful cherry paneling in the dining room were all costly extras."

Carolyn flicked through the papers on her lap and pulled out a photograph. "I made a copy of a picture of the house taken in the twenties. Thought you might enjoy seeing it."

David took the photograph and examined it. It was in black and white, of course. It definitely pictured his house, only it had a wooden structure at one end. He recognized it as the cabin sitting over on the edge of the woods.

Pointing to the addition, he asked, "I wonder why they moved this part of the building?"

Carolyn shrugged. "My guess would be that styles and priorities changed. Back in the fifties, people were not so interested in the authenticity of the architecture. They were, if anything, more interested in modernizing things."

Handing back the photo, David said, "So, what else have you for me today?"

Carolyn handed him two sheets of paper containing architect's drawings of floor plans. "I printed out a plan for each floor trying to accommodate your requests." Pointing with a pencil to the one he held on top, she said, "Because of the huge size of the wing containing the kitchen and the small bedrooms, it is possible to create a combined kitchen and family room in those areas. I was able to position the fireplace against this wall.

"I thought you might want to consider having a combination washroom, laundry and mudroom where the two small rooms are now. Any children could come in this door and get rid of their winter clothes easily before coming into the kitchen. I also thought there was room to include a small workroom or study for your wife. The light would be sufficient and your wife would have a place to pursue her interests."

Carolyn watched him out of the corner of her eye as she gave him the information, not sure whether he would mind her reference to children and a wife. However, he seemed unconcerned.

He continued to study the plan, questioning her about the other rooms on each floor and the insertion of bathrooms where they were needed. They discussed the basement and exactly how he saw it being used. Finally, Carolyn stood. "I'll leave these ideas for you to consider. Nothing is carved in stone. You can make any request at this point and I will try to accommodate you. However, before we go any farther, I think you should discuss the financial side of this project with my father. I have included a general rundown on the costs. I can be more specific as soon as you decide whether you want to contact us for this job. If you are free this evening after supper, my dad and I would be happy to sit down with you in our office and work out a contract."

David rose to his feet. Indicating the papers in his hand, he said, "I'm impressed. I didn't think you could possibly have this much done in so short a time." He couldn't help but be charmed by the flush of pleasure that colored her face. "I'll spend the rest of the day studying these and making notes. I would like to meet your father. Where is your office?"

Heading for the verandah steps, Carolyn called over her shoulder, "It's in our home. Just drive through town to the drug store, turn right, and we live in the white house on the next corner. You can't miss it. How about eight o'clock?"

"That's fine," David said and settled back down to watch her walk to the van. No workboots today, he thought. Sneakers instead. She sure does wear jeans well. She really is an attractive woman, far too attractive.


David gulped down a quick breakfast of cornflakes while drinking coffee in his shambles of a kitchen. Looking gloomily about the room, he wondered how he'd overlooked it for so long. He was going to insist that this area be tackled first whether Ms. Thompson agreed or not.

He'd managed with only a microwave oven, a plug-in tea kettle and a few plates, glasses, cups and pans; making a meal when necessary. Normally, he drove the few miles into town to enjoy breakfast. Today, however, all the male members of the Thompson clan, except Jim Thompson, were coming out to give the house the once-over.

David had found Jim Thompson to be straightforward and practical. Carolyn and he had already sketched out a fairly clear outline of what needed to be done and what such work would cost. They had in each case where quality was concerned, given a lower and higher cost, explaining that for example, one could have a satisfactory bathroom for a fairly reasonable cost, or one could have glass and marble shower stalls and a Jacuzzi for considerably more. In the end, he was given both low and high estimates on costs. But Carolyn would not hear of him signing a contract until all three men came out and looked at the house.

David knew that this was completely unnecessary. He had caught the look of surprise on Jim's face when Carolyn said, "I think we should wait until the men in the family have looked at the house. They might see something I've overlooked. And of course, they can answer your questions more specifically. Besides, each has a creative streak that you might find interesting."

He hadn't been able to stop the surge of resentment he felt when she had so cleverly poked at his prejudice. Nor could he avoid thinking that her own indignation, although hidden carefully from her father, brought a glitter to her very eloquent eyes and a flush to her cheeks. *Why couldn't she look like a construction worker instead of a long-legged temptress?* That thought irritated him even more. He was not interested in temptation. He wanted a serious relationship.

The rumble of vans brought him back to the present. Quickly rinsing out his cup and bowl, he hurried outside to meet the males of the Thompson clan.

Out of the first van, labeled *Ben Thompson Plumbing*, stepped a tall fair-haired young man who introduced himself as Ben. From another van, this time labeled *Andrew Thompson Electrical*, an equally tall but dark-haired man with a ponytail, older than Ben but just as confident, strolled over and greeted him with a strong handshake. The final man to step from his truck was Mike, in charge of construction. He was the tallest of the lot and eye-to-eye with David. He was obviously the oldest brother, his dark hair streaked with grey and trimmed a very proper length.

After introducing himself to David, Mike gave each brother a print-out of the plans agreed on the night before and suggested they take a look around. David had a notion that the older brother disapproved of this entire exercise but was making sure that the others knew what was expected of them.

David left them and because it was to be another incredibly beautiful spring day, decided to continue working in his garden. As he guided the rototiller through what was to become his vegetable garden, he wondered where the fair Carolyn was at that moment. Where had the words *fair Carolyn* come from? he wondered, as if she was a princess and the men crawling about his house were her knights. And, he thought, unable to stop himself from carrying the idea to its conclusion, why was it he felt like the evil baron?

It wasn't long before the three men wandered down to where he was working, notes in hand. Turning off the rototiller, David offered lemonade and led them to the verandah. A handy thing, a verandah, he thought as he passed out the beverages. It created a friendly ambiance that might just tip the balance in his favor and get a nod of approval from big brother Mike.

The three men settled; Ben on the steps, Andy leaning against the railing and Mike on the other chair. For a few moments, they discussed David's love of gardening and then he asked, "Well, what do you think? Any suggestions?"

He expected Mike to answer, but Ben, with what David suspected was his usual enthusiasm, piped up, "As usual, Carolyn has done a brilliant job. The architects of this world don't know what they're missing." Before David could ask him what he meant, Ben continued. "I think the way she's planned the piping is a plumber's dream, particularly as the walls will be open and the basement new. It makes it even easier that the previous owner put in a very large septic system.

"I have one suggestion. Carolyn said the room just beyond the mudroom could be a lady's study or workroom. I wonder if it wouldn't be wise to put in a small sink. Then if the lady likes to paint, for example, it would be handy for cleaning brushes. You might include a fan in case she uses oil paints." Then turning bright blue eyes that the entire clan seemed to be blessed with, he asked, "Does she paint?"

David couldn't tell from the innocence of his expression if he was pulling his leg or quite sincere but Mike piped up, "You might want to consider lighting that would suit an artist or someone sewing. My wife's a quilter and she bugged me until I found just the right light."

Deciding not to confess he had no idea what the lady in question might prefer, he nodded in agreement. "I think both ideas are good. Then, if she develops either hobby, she will be pleased. I would also like the room wired to accommodate a computer with the same fail-safe devices you'll be putting in the study for me."

At that point, Mike suggested that David tour the house with them starting in the basement so that each could answer any questions he might have. Again, David was suspicious. Surely they didn't take the time and trouble to do this with every client. He sensed the fine hand of Carolyn Thompson behind the exercise but decided to go along with the tour.

When they finished and were about to leave, Ben noticed the newspaper with the tennis club advertisement sitting on the verandah table. He pointed to it and asked, "You interested in tennis?"

"Very," replied David.

"I play whenever I can spare the time. I'm going over there tonight. Why don't you meet me at the court about seven?"

David couldn't agree fast enough. He'd enjoy a few sets with Ben. Just as he was about to wave them off, Ben yelled over his shoulder, "Carolyn asked if she could come over to see you about two o'clock. I think she has some ideas for your kitchen."

Kitchen? he thought. For a moment he felt just a little bit uneasy. Would she expect him to know exactly what he wanted? For all his dreams of a warm friendly area, he realized that he had few ideas about the specifics. Naturally, it would have to have a sink and appliances. But what if she wanted him to decide the arrangement of these things? He'd never even thought about that.

Realizing that Ben was still waiting for a reply, he yelled, "Sure."

He turned and headed back to his garden. As he started his rototiller again, he thought that if he heard what a marvelous job Carolyn was doing just once more, he'd scream.

He managed two laps back and forth with the rototiller

before the hateful memories of Linda Morrison started to crowd his mind. He'd been so young when he started university, a real geek. And yet he'd managed, all on his own, to get a summer job on a road crew. It was just his bad luck that Linda had been the forewoman.

She'd been a good-looking woman, dark-haired with pleasant features except for the meanest brown eyes in creation. She'd taken one look at him and decided to take all her frustrations out on him. With hindsight, he realized that she must have fought hard to attain her position. It would have been necessary for her to outperform, outmaneuver and outswear absolutely every man she'd worked with to get her job, and certainly some of the guys on the road crew were no angels. The fact that she was a widow with a child had given her a drive that many of the men resented.

David paused for a moment, reflecting that it was only now that he could find any reason for her excessive cruelty to him. All her resentment toward the men she had struggled against seemed to find its outlet on his innocent head. She'd criticized, ridiculed and ordered him to undertake every rotten task she could think of. It had gotten so bad that finally the rest of the work crew rebelled, warning that she'd better stop or they would report her.

Shoving the rototiller ahead, he plowed up and down the garden, still seeing her image stomping around in heavy boots and a hard hat; belittling, sneering and doing her best to make his life miserable. Even though his tuition had been paid by scholarships, he had to endure her persecution because he desperately needed the job to cover his expenses.

It was no wonder, he reflected, that Carolyn, Miss Perfection herself if her brothers were to be believed, got under his skin. Although, in all fairness, he had to admit that she didn't have cruel eyes. Nor was she anything like Linda.

Carolyn drove up to the house just after lunch, quite unaware that her brothers had picked up the notion from their father that David had little confidence in a woman doing renovations. Nor did she know that they had behaved like overanxious big brothers all morning.

Carrying a pile of catalogs and a folder with several mock-ups of the kitchen, she headed for the house until she heard someone talking. Following the voice, she walked behind the house toward the large garden plot to find David busy playing with the cat while raking the freshly rototilled earth. Every second or third time he dug in the rake, he shot a little bit of earth at the cat who crouched down comically, tail thrashing, ready to fling himself up in the air to catch each small missile.

"He's a good baseball player as well as a mouser, I see," she observed with a smile and thought, and you're not nearly as arrogant when you play with your cat.

David turned and grinned. "Charlie is an exceptional cat. He loves to play. If he's bored, he makes up games."

Noticing that her arms were full, he took the pile of catalogs. "Wow, you really intend to work."

"I thought that you might be anxious to have the kitchen and family room done right away. Possibly the laundry room and little washroom as well. Then, you could at least be comfortable."

With that, she led him to the verandah and through the door to the kitchen. When she placed her folder on the old table, he put the catalogs beside it and pulled up two chairs.

"I drafted a number of plans for this area. Not to dictate to you what you should have," she hastened to explain. "But sometimes, when you see plans for a space, it helps you to discern what you really like."

As David placed the large pile of catalogs on the table, he frowned. This wasn't what he'd expected. He assumed she would present him with the final decision. The fact that she acted in a way he hadn't expected confused him.

Trying to hide this fact, he took the other chair. "Okay. Let's see your suggestions."

David studied the plans for quite a while. She was nothing if not creative, he thought, since each of the three mock-ups she'd prepared were quite different. Finally, he selected one particular set of drawings.

He was impressed with their excellence, and in fairness to her felt obliged to say, "These are first class." Placing his selection on top of the others, he went on, "I like them all, but I think this design is best. I like having this island with the sink between the kitchen and family room. A person could watch small children while he or she worked."

Carolyn leaned forward to study his choice and as she did, strands of loose hair fell forward, releasing a scent that reminded him of wildflowers. For a second, David was stunned by the fragrance, unable to focus on anything else.

Unaware that she'd lost his attention, she pulled the catalogs toward her. Selecting four of them, she said, "I thought that, if you had time, you could look at these pictures of various kitchens. They might give you an idea about the kind of doors you would like for the cupboards. There are also illustrations of counter material. I've written out labels and attached them to the books so you know where the different materials are. There are also books about windows."

David flicked through the first book, startled at the variety of kitchen doors available. He knew that he would hate this project. He realized, suddenly, that although he said he wanted to be part of the decision making, reading through all these catalogs would drive him up the wall. But he wasn't ready to admit that to Carolyn.

He turned his attention to the window catalogs. "Do you want me to study these too?"

This time, she shook her head. "No, not exactly. Of course, it depends."

Now what exactly does that mean? "Depends on what?"

Carolyn looked cautious. "Well, I thought you'd want to retain the basic style of the house. Right?"

"I said so at the beginning."

"In that case, you really are stuck with the same kind of windows you already have." As he opened his mouth to speak, she rushed on. "If you want to keep the brickwork design above the windows, then they have to be custom-built and double-hung so they'll fit into the exact space of the old ones."

Pulling the catalogs toward her, she began to open the books at specific pages. "I've marked each catalog so you can view the options. They don't vary much except in the kind of framing and whether you want large or small panes." Quickly, she set the books open for his perusal.

David studied her. She wore a soft pink sweatshirt that emphasized her delicate complexion. As she arranged the books, he noticed her long eyelashes and the slender line of her neck. Today her hair was pulled back in a pink wiggly-cloth-elastic-thing girls seemed to favor. He found himself wondering how it would feel to run his fingers through her hair.

She looked up at him, a question in her eyes. He realized he hadn't heard a word she'd said. What on earth did he think he was doing, mooning over this woman's hair instead of paying attention? Inspiration hit. "I think we should go outside and look at the windows again."

As Carolyn followed David outside, she wondered what had happened. Why did she think that for some reason, they hadn't been communicating?

Carolyn gave the tennis ball a real blast over the net. Her partner Dan yelled, "Hey, you want to change the rules?"

Carolyn apologized. "Sorry Dan, I was thinking about work. I won't do it again."

Annoyed, she tried to concentrate on the game. She and Dan played whenever they had a chance. They were well-matched but had decided that they enjoyed a good game rather than a contest. They knew their strengths and weaknesses and lazily challenged each other rather than seeing how quickly they could be demolished.

Carolyn liked the easy pace of the game. It helped her unwind. And with Dan, she could be herself. She was sorry that things hadn't worked out between them. They dated for nearly a year before finally admitting that, although they liked and admired each other, there was simply no spark between them. Their relationship would remain platonic. They kept up their tennis games and occasionally helped each other when they needed an escort.

Dan was a good-looking man, very fair, tall, and quite intelligent. Two years before, he'd purchased the local veterinary practice and had been successful in keeping the area farmers and small animal owners as clients.

Each of them understood the other's professional re-
sponsibilities.

Their final volley ended and they left the courts. As
Carolyn packed her racquet, she heard a shout of laughter from the court farthest away. She recognized Ben's
voice as he yelled, "Gotcha, Barbie. You'll have to move
faster than that."

She paused for a moment to watch the action. Ben
was playing with Sara, but who was the man with Barbara? It took her a moment to recognize David Reid. He
was good. Then she realized something else. He was
being very attentive to Barbara. Actually, he seemed to
be flirting. She couldn't quite hear what was being said,
but she could make out the intonation of their conversation. Turning away, she grinned to herself. So David
had started his search for a wife. And he liked cute little
blonds. Well, it wouldn't be that easy for him. She was
fairly sure that Ben was just as interested in Barbara.

David bowed deeply to his partner's applause after
he'd slammed one into Ben's corner. Amongst the laughter and catcalls from those watching, David caught the
ball for his serve. It was then he happened to glance
toward the clubhouse door. A tall man was walking toward its steps, his arm draped around the shoulders of a
dark-haired woman with long, slim legs wearing a saucy
pink tennis skirt guaranteed to increase his heart rate.
Then, his eyes focused on a ring of pink fabric caught
at the top of her ponytail. It took him only a second to
realize the woman was Carolyn.

*Chapter Three*

David woke to the sounds of trucks and voices. Looking at his watch, he was surprised to see that it was just 7:00. Dressing quickly in jeans and a sweatshirt, he hurried outside. He was in time to see Carolyn stepping out of her van and walking over to her brother Mike. As David reached them, Mike turned to answer a question shouted at him by a burly man removing the chains on a flatbed carrying a bulldozer.

Carolyn smiled. "Well, I hope you're ready for noise and confusion. Mike's team will start by digging a trench around the house's foundation. Then they'll place the steel beams you see on that flatbed coming up the road under the house itself."

The bulldozer rumbled past them, drowning out her next words. Touching her arm, David motioned toward the verandah. "Do you have time for coffee?"

Carolyn glanced around and seemed satisfied with the activity. "Sure. I need to talk to you anyway."

David led the way into the kitchen and filled the coffeemaker. As they waited for the coffee, Carolyn searched for the right words to bring up the next subject on her agenda. She was sure it wasn't going to be easy. Finally, she blurted out, "David, you won't be able to stay in the house for the next few weeks."

He turned toward her, an objection already forming, but she continued before he could get the words out. "The minute the trench is dug and they are ready to lift the house, the power will be disconnected. Ben is coming today to disconnect the plumbing."

Carolyn felt uncomfortable. She'd been sure Mike had already made it clear David must move. It was only the previous night that she'd discovered Mike hadn't told David that he couldn't use the house while they lifted it.

From David's expression she knew he was not pleased. Darn Mike, she thought. He didn't usually screw up over such an important item. Folding his arms across his chest, David asked sarcastically, "And just where do you suggest I stay for the next few weeks?"

Watching him nervously, Carolyn suggested, "Well, you could stay in the cabin. A previous owner must have thought of using it as a cottage. It's wired for power. You could use one of our generators until the hydro runs a line to it or even oil lamps. We can set up a pump to bring water up from the lake. There is a sink and counter there and you can drink bottled water." Then a devil of mischief made her add, "Of course, it's possible the lake is warm enough to wash in and there is an old outhouse behind the cabin."

She had to choke down laughter at his indignant expression. "Have you looked at that old pile of wood?" he demanded. "There's a wasp nest the size of a football inside."

"Fear not," she grinned, "We'll get you a portable toilet. There's one coming for the men. I'll order another for you."

That's just great, David thought. Portable bathroom and oil lamps. And darn it, she's enjoying this. Glaring at her, he asked, "And if I don't want to live in the cabin?"

"You could buy a tent or go to a motel."

David groaned, "I need some coffee." Grabbing two mugs, he filled them, offered milk and sugar and headed for the verandah. Instead of sitting down, she said, "Thanks for the coffee. Think about what you want to do. I'll be back in a few moments. I want to check on everyone."

David watched sourly as she sashayed off to meet Ben's van. She had no business looking so darned sexy. This morning she wore a soft turquoise sweatshirt and a tight pair of blue jeans. Her hair was looped up at the back of her neck. And of course, she wore a pair of workboots.

After finishing his coffee he rooted around in his fridge and found an orange. Peeling it, he considered his options. He knew he was being unreasonable when he said he wanted to stay in the house. He knew the dust would mess up his computer and the noise would drive him crazy. He also knew that if one of the brothers had asked, he would have moved without argument. So why was he being such a miserable cuss over this? he wondered. Why did he let Carolyn Thompson get under his skin?

With a sigh of resignation, he headed out to the cabin. Stepping inside and peering around, he had to admit it wasn't so bad. In fact, it would probably be warmer and dryer than the house. He noticed the windows even had screens. Carolyn was right. Someone had thought about using it for a cottage.

There was a cupboard with a sink in it. Looking around, he saw that there were indeed wall plugs and a light hanging from the ceiling. The place needed a good vacuuming and the windows washed but otherwise, it seemed okay. He could bring over his bed, desk and the few belongings he needed.

The screen door opened and Carolyn stepped in. "Well, what do you think?"

David looked about him grimly, "It needs a good vacuuming and the windows cleaned. But I guess if you can arrange some power, water and a portable toilet, I can manage."

He couldn't help but notice her relief. "I'll arrange for a crew to come over to vacuum and clean the windows right away," she said.

"You don't have to do that."

"But . . ."

"I'm quite capable of cleaning up. I'll go into the hardware store and get a wet/dry vacuum. I'll need one anyway. I'll get cleaning materials too." He grinned at her look of amazement. "Don't worry, Carolyn. I do know how to clean a house as well as quite a few other interesting things."

With a look of disbelief, she shook her head and watched as he headed to the pickup. Amazing, she thought. An academic who can actually thread a needle, so to speak.


Carolyn left the site to check on other matters. When she returned at 4:00, she wandered over to the cabin. The sound of a generator surprised her. Walking inside, she discovered David washing a window. The floor was clean and the sundry cobwebs were gone. In the corner, she spied an old rolled-up carpet. In the middle of the floor were new boxes whose markings made it clear that they contained dishes, pans and flatware. Beside the boxes sat a portable heater.

David watched as Carolyn inspected his boxes. Her expression of surprise made all his hard work worth it. "Well, what do you think?"

She looked around. "The place looks really great. It's in much better condition than the house. But I told you that we'd supply a generator."

"I decided I should have one anyway. Remember the ice storm of '98? Many people would have been thankful to have one at the time."

Carolyn wandered over to the rug and boxes. She touched the one containing dishes with her toe. "You'll be more comfortable here than you were in the house. Looked like you only had one dish for yourself and another for the cat."

"Just looking ahead. I'm sure I'm going to have visitors, especially family. Thought I might as well start picking up the things I'll need to make this a guest house. When you've finished the house, you can fix this place up."

Carolyn's heart sank at this. She really thought the cabin should be returned to the house. Half the houses in the countryside had similar attachments. Moreover, the cabin was perfectly proportioned for the house.

"You seem to have reservations, Carolyn."

She shook her head. There was no use starting an argument. She'd wait and see what happened; maybe he'd change his mind.

Turning to the door, Carolyn said, "I'll get some of

the guys to bring over your things. However, you'd better pack your electronic equipment."

A week later, David turned off his computer and looked out the window. He liked this cabin. It had really great windows. From his desk, he could see in three directions.

Spring had cooled down considerably and was far more seasonable. It had rained for three days while the men raised the house. In spite of this, even the basement pad was down and the walls constructed. Tomorrow, they would remove the long steel beams. It had been fascinating to watch while they inched the house up in the air using small pneumatic jacks. To his amazement, not one thing in the house had been broken.

Oddly enough, he hadn't seen much of Carolyn. There had been times when her van was there, but she never came over. She hadn't even been at the tennis court on the nights the rain had eased off.

And, he thought gloomily, I've made very little headway in my search for a wife.

David went outside. It was warmer this morning and there was a pleasant breeze that dispersed the mosquitos that reigned supreme for several weeks each spring. Down one side of the ridge, on which the house and cabin were situated, was an old orchard. The trees were a mass of blossom. Taking a deep breath of the soft warm air, David decided it was a good time to inspect them. Just after he moved into the house, he'd pruned the trees. Growing up around his parents' nursery had given him a general idea when the trees should be trimmed and how to care for them.

As he wandered under the branches, squinting up through the mass of pink-white blossoms, he had the strangest sensation. In one way, the bright blue sky behind the blossoms lifted his spirits and seemed to confirm that he had been right to get out of the rat race. At the same time, the fresh smells of spring, the blossoms' scent and the rich odor of the earth stirred a feeling of restlessness; as if things were not complete.

A branch cracked. Turning, he discovered Carolyn walking down the hill. Strangely, she seemed to float toward him between the row of blossoming trees. David shut his eyes and opened them again. She was close enough now for him to see that her hair was loose, floating behind her. She wore a soft pink sweater and a flowing denim skirt accompanied by her pair of big, clumping workboots.

David groaned inwardly as his vision disappeared and Carolyn the contractor reached him.

Carolyn waved her clipboard. "Hi. I'm going into Smithboro to select the flooring for your kitchen. I wondered if you'd like to come?"

David frowned, still slightly bewildered by the few seconds of pure romanticism that had just passed. "I thought I'd made it clear that I wanted hardwood."

"But there are many tones and finishes to choose from. You can also use synthetic or real wood. I thought you might find it informative to talk to the man at Dubek's Building Supplies in Smithboro. I have other things to do there while you speak to him, and I need to return by four o'clock." When David didn't say anything, she said, "I know it's short notice. But it's such a nice day I decided I couldn't stand to work inside. If today's not suitable for you, then let me know a time that's good and I'll set up an appointment with Sandy Dubek for you."

David took another look around at the blossoms and the sparkling lake below them. She was right. It was too nice a day to stay inside. "Okay," he said. "Give me a few minutes to clean up."

Just as he began to climb back up the hill, she touched his arm. "Wait. Listen."

David turned to her, wondering what he should listen to. She stood, transfixed, the sun sifting down through the leaves and blossoms, touching her fair skin and emphasizing the expression of pure rapture on her face. Her blue eyes were unfocused, her head tilted to one side. "Listen," she whispered.

All David could hear was a cacophony of spring birds each outdoing the other when suddenly, a sweet whistle cut through the sound. She held up her finger. A whistle answered from another side of the orchard. "It's the orioles. They always come back at this time of year. I didn't know there were any nesting up here."

She hurried ahead of him, dark tresses massed over her shoulders and tumbling down her back, her head cocked to one side as she followed the whistling. A wayward thought crossed David's mind: Carolyn fit his own romantic notion of the woman he wanted for a wife. Frowning, David cut the thought off before it could take root and concentrated on her big boots clumping over the fresh grasses and wild violets.

The town of Smithboro was a thirty-five-minute drive from Stewart's Falls. Because of its larger size, it offered a greater variety of products. Dubek's was one of the best, always used by Thompson Builders.

Carolyn had asked David to accompany her and pick out the flooring because she sensed he would reject anything she suggested. She still hadn't figured out why.

Uneasily, she glanced over at him. He'd changed into jeans and a white T-shirt, and tossed a denim jacket in the back. She'd been right when she'd thought he had an aura about him. She could feel his energy even on her side of the van. It seemed to be reaching out and taking in all the sights and sounds around him. Even creepier was the sense that he was somehow reaching her, creating a tension that she couldn't quite identify.

Uncomfortable with herself, she decided on conversation. Glancing at him, she asked, "David, what did you do before you moved here?"

"I developed wireless computer chips and successfully established a company to market them. It was the right technology at the right time."

"What company was that?"

She sensed he was uncomfortable giving an answer. Finally, he said, "DR Electronics Ltd."

She looked at him in surprise. "Wow, I've read about DR Electronic's in the business section many times."

When he made no response, she decided to dig a little more. "Have you left the company?"

She could see David shift awkwardly in his seat. Finally, he said, "I sold it last January."

She waited for more, and when he wasn't forthcoming, she asked, "Why?"

"The life of an innovator and executive takes all your waking hours. You don't have time to think, to socialize, to have friends or family. I finally took a holiday last autumn and stayed with my brother and his family. He has a lovely wife and two great kids. I was very aware of what was missing in my life. Also, my mother asked me a question."

She glanced at him again, waiting for the question. She could tell that he didn't really like to talk about this. Finally, he said, "She asked me if I was happy. If my accomplishments were enough for me."

"And . . ."

She's not going to stop until I've spilled my guts, thought David. A little voice told him he needn't answer her question, but for some reason, he felt compelled. It was aggravating, but he found that he wanted her to understand.

"I came to the conclusion that work was not enough. To start with, I was getting bored. There weren't as many challenges. Also, if I continued, I knew that I would have to break new territory, and that takes eighteen-hour days. You literally wake up and find that your mind is racing with each problem. There is never any rest or recreation for that matter. One becomes inwardly focused and antisocial. I decided I'd had enough, so I sold."

He looked at her now. She should be satisfied. She'd gotten all the answers. He was surprised to see that she seemed to be pondering his answers. He sensed that she was frowning.

"What will you do with your time now?" Her question interrupted his musing.

"I've accepted a part-time teaching position at Durham University. But my first love is math. I want to spend some time concentrating on the latest ideas in mathematics."

Just then, they wheeled into the parking lot of Dubek's Building Supplies.


David was glowering and he knew it. Sandy Dubek had discussed in lengthy detail every kind of flooring he should consider; pre-finished solid oak plank, oak tongue-and-groove plank, maple plank or tongue-and-groove maple, and several kinds of laminates guaranteed to outlast the wood. How did *she* expect him to know which wood he wanted? He wasn't the expert. He just wanted a kitchen with a wooden floor, real or laminate. Where was she anyway?

He looked around the large store and finally spotted a flash of pink over by the tile section. He took a step toward the tile section and then stopped. Sure as anything, if he went over there, she'd make him decide whether he wanted plain tile, flowered tile or Italian tile. Grinding his teeth, he went back to the sample woods and laminates.

Glancing around, he saw that no one was watching. He began to play with the samples, constructing a small tower by putting them on their sides. He was just placing the final sample flat on top when an amused voice said right at his shoulder, "Is that the one you want?"

Startled, he jumped and the samples came clattering down, skittering across the small table where they were kept and falling to the floor; each piece sounding like a gunshot. People stopped and turned to stare.

David stood, furious with himself, the wood pieces, and her. Before he could move, she was kneeling, sweeping up the wooden pieces and beginning to place them in order back on the table.

Sensing that David had almost reached meltdown, Carolyn carefully organized the samples and waited. When she thought it might be safe to speak, she asked, "Have you made a decision?"

Out of the corner of her eye, she watched his face and realized that it had not been the smartest question in the world.

He leaned toward her, nose to nose. "No, I have not," he snapped. "And I don't know why I should. After all, you're the expert. That's what I'm paying you for. You're supposed to make these decisions."

She didn't budge an inch. Staring him right in the eye,

she asked, "Really? And would you have agreed if I'd told you that you were to have a certain kind and color of floor?"

David opened his mouth to speak and then honesty made him reconsider. Shoving his hands in his trouser pockets, he shrugged. "Probably not."

Deciding that there was no time like the present to try and discover just why he resented her making the decisions he was paying her to make, Carolyn asked, "Why, David?"

Rubbing his hand across his jaw, he eyed her carefully. What was it about her that really bugged him? Was it that she never backed down? Like now. She wanted an answer. With a weary shrug, he mumbled, "You choose," and walked away.


David leaned against her van wondering how he was going to get out of the hole he had just dug himself into. He didn't want to fight with Carolyn. Actually, he admired her. She was clearheaded, honest, and hardworking. She certainly kept him on his toes. Why couldn't he just admit he didn't know what he wanted?

He saw her exit the store carrying two different bundles of wood. Behind her Sandy Dubek appeared carrying another four. Without a word, David opened the door of the van, took the bundles from them, and piled them on the van's floor.

David watched Carolyn turn to Sandy and give him one of her million-dollar smiles. "Thanks, Sandy. We'll bring the samples back when we're finished. See you."

Turning to David, she explained, "I realized that we think quite differently. You're a concept man. When you say you want a kitchen and family room with a wooden floor, you're thinking of the idea. I, on the other hand, think concretely. For me, it's easy to imagine such a room. I know immediately which material and color I want. Therefore, I decided that it would make much more sense to you if we took the samples home and spread them out on the floor, both in daylight and in the evening."

What could David say? He knew that he had just been given a gracious out for his surly behavior. Reaching up, he pulled down the van door and slammed it shut. Turning to her, he smiled, a conciliatory one he hoped, and said, "You know, I think you may be right. C'mon. I'm buying lunch."

When they were in the van, David surprised Carolyn by saying, "It's much too nice to eat in Smithboro. Do you have time for lunch at Allen's Marina?"

If it meant getting their relationship back on an even keel, she'd gladly take a few hours off. "I'd love that. It's a perfect day to eat by the lake. And their windows are screened which means no mosquitos."

He smiled at that and settled back comfortably, happy to be driven, satisfied that he had managed to ease the tension between them.

Carolyn took her time. She needed to think. She knew that she could easily have settled the matter of the kitchen. All she had to do was make several models. She'd done it often enough in the past.

She recalled the model she'd made for James and memories came flooding back. She'd only been twenty, an architectural student at the University of Toronto and desperately in love with him. They'd met at the campus art gallery early in the season and connected right away, both enjoying the work of the resident artist. When James had asked her to have supper with him, she was hooked.

At first, it had been like a fairy tale. James had taken her dining, found interesting movies for them to see and, she realized now, spent a great deal of time airing the same theories he expounded in his fine arts classes. She, on the other hand, had been dazzled by the fact that such a handsome, clever man found her attractive and interesting.

Slowly, though, as she had become more involved with her studies, tension had built. James was not happy when she said she was too busy to go out. When they were together, he showed little interest in her projects and, in fact, in the subtlest manner, belittled them. But she, poor fool, had ignored little digs, still floating in a romantic haze, certain that theirs was a match made in heaven.

The exams before Christmas had been a stressful time for both of them. James had been in a temper because he had extra grading to do. She'd been exhausted because not only did she have exams to write, but a major project to finish. To add to that pressure, she'd decided to make a special gift for James for his birthday on the nineteenth of December.

In typical James fashion, his birthday had to be an event. A well-chosen group of friends and acquaintances were invited to a party at his fashionable Cabbage Town row house. This tiny house, built in an area settled by the Irish in the late 1800s, was one of five that had been renovated brilliantly by a local architect.

Carolyn loved these houses; they appealed to every creative instinct she had. The exteriors had been renewed with careful accuracy so that it seemed as if one stepped back into nineteenth-century Toronto on entering the tiny street.

Carolyn arrived at James's party, dressed in a truly

elegant, black velvet gown and carrying a large rectangular box wrapped gaily for the occasion. Free at last of exams and projects, she enjoyed the evening immensely. James was busy flitting from guest to guest so Carolyn spent ages talking to the architect who'd renovated the houses.

When it came time to read the cards people brought, James took a seat where he would be seen most easily, and Carolyn sat beside him, like some silly handmaiden, and presented him the cards. Finally, there was only Carolyn's gift remaining.

Carolyn hadn't thought it inappropriate for her to give him a gift, after all, they had been together with these people socially on more than one occasion. However, it suddenly occurred to her that she might have waited until they were alone. Somewhat shyly, she'd handed him the box saying, "I didn't bring a card. Since it's Christmas, I thought you might add this to your decorations."

Everyone leaned forward as James untied the large bow, tore off the paper, and lifted the lid off the box. Inside was a model of his street, the detail of each house accurate down to the individual door knockers. All were gaily decorated for Christmas. James lifted it up and held it out for people to see, then said, "Carolyn's been playing with her scissors and paste again. Isn't it quaint."

Carolyn heard very little more and missed the guests' words of praise. Instead, she took the model from his hands, moved to the old-fashioned fireplace mantle, and placed it where she intended it to sit. She hoped that no one else had heard the disparaging undertone of James's words and was trying very hard to stifle the tears that fought to surface.

She spent the rest of the party hiding in the kitchen, busily setting out food, wishing with all her heart she'd never thought of making the model. It was only when the architect had tracked her down that she'd begun to feel better. He'd said, "I'm impressed Carolyn. Where'd you learn to do such fine work? I bet there isn't one dimension out of place."

She smiled at that. "I've been making models for years. Also, I'm an architectural student."

He raised his eyebrows in surprise. "I should have realized that after talking to you earlier. You were so well informed. James has no idea what a treasure he has in you. Nor, I suspect, does he have any idea the skill or time that went into making that model. I'd like to commission you to make one for me, though not with a Christmas theme. You can construct it when the school term is over. If you need a summer job, I'd be happy to discuss it with you in April."

But it was not to be. The following day, her father had a heart attack. Shattered, she'd phoned James with the news, hoping for support. She'd received none and had left Toronto brokenhearted and fearful for her father's life.

Anger pumped through Carolyn's veins at the memory, startling her with its intensity. She became aware that her breathing had intensified and that her hands were clamped tightly to the steering wheel. Slowly, she eased her grip and at the same time, tried to slow her breathing. She was stunned at her reaction. She'd no idea how deeply she still resented James's treatment of her. No wonder she found it hard to help David when all that anger was still seething inside her.

Glancing at David, she was relieved to find him relaxed, whistling softly to himself and looking out the window. As she turned down the side road to the marina, he said, "I'm really enjoying this. I rarely get a chance to sit back and watch the scenery."

Reaching the parking lot behind the marina, Carolyn parked the van and they got out. To one side of the moorings and boat racks was the restaurant located above the marina office. Climbing wooden stairs, they reached the entrance.

David opened the door for Carolyn and followed her in. They were greeted by a smiling young waitress who led them to a table by a screened window. As they were seated, Carolyn turned to the waitress and said, "Hi, Cindy. I didn't know you were working here."

Cindy gave them both a sparkling smile, handed them menus, and said, "I've been here a week. Great, eh?"

"But I thought you'd be in the kitchen creating something fabulous for us to eat."

"Later in the season I'll be cooking. This is a pleasant change."

Carolyn realized that she hadn't introduced Cindy. "David, I'd like you to meet Cindy Howard. She's training to be a chef at a college in Toronto."

Carolyn was amused to see that David was quite taken by Cindy, but then she was a very attractive young woman. Cindy had a delicate heart-shaped face, snapping brown eyes, and curly hair the color of light taffy. Slender and of average height, she wore her black and white waitress's uniform with style. Carolyn could easily imagine her having her own cooking show on television.

Once their order was taken, David asked, "What's going to happen next to my house?"

"Well," Carolyn explained, "Since you say money is no object, and you are anxious for us to finish as soon as possible, I've hired extra workmen to begin to clear out all the old plaster and any insulation that's under it.

We'll be setting up chutes from some of the windows, and the material will be sent down the chutes into garbage dumpsters. Actually, the chutes and dumpsters should be in place when we get back. The men start tomorrow under my supervision."

Cindy returned with glasses of water, flatware and table napkins. As she set them down, David said, "Carolyn tells me you're training to be a chef." Cindy nodded. Every time she came to the table, he asked more about her training.

Carolyn smiled. David was so obvious about his sudden interest in Cindy. Carolyn was sure that David was checking her out as possible wife material, or at least, as an expert on kitchens.

Near the end of the meal, Cindy asked Carolyn, "Do you know if the tennis crowd is going to help make scenery for the summer play?"

Every year, some of the citizens of Stewart's Falls put on a musical or a farce to raise money for the local hospital. It was great fun and involved people of all ages. Those who didn't want to act or sing often volunteered their talents behind the scenes. Over time, it had become the habit of the tennis club to assist with the scenery.

"I'll ask around," Carolyn told Cindy. "When are you going to start work on the scenery?"

"We thought that the crew should be organized and ready to start within the next week or so."

Carolyn was amused when David piped up, "What does one have to do? I'd like to help."

Cindy gave him a delighted smile. "Well, we'd love to have you. You'll probably be given a can of paint and a brush and told to daub green bits for leaves on the scenery, or a roller and told to paint a wall. It's all great fun."

"Will you be painting?" asked David.

"Nope, I've a lead in the farce. However, we all get together at the end of the evening and go over to the coffee shop."

Carolyn could see the wheels turning in David's head as he paid the bill and they left. Here was another woman for him to consider on his search for a wife. Had David ever heard of love at first sight or plain and simple attraction? Did he really think it was just a matter of whether one could cook? It would serve him right if he fell like a load of bricks for someone who couldn't boil water and hated kids.

When they returned to his house with the samples, Carolyn had to leave. As she was about to step into the van, David asked, "Where can I get a hard hat and the correct kind of workboots? I might as well be useful until the mess is cleared up outside. Then I can work on the grounds. Anyway, I want to help."

Carolyn opened her mouth, about to object, then thought better of it. She could tell from the determined glint in his eyes that she'd be wasting her time. With a sigh, she told him she was sure she had a hard hat. He could buy his boots and safety glasses in town.

As she drove off, she groused to herself. All she needed was another person underfoot. It was going to be hard enough with the part-time people she'd hired, without having to instruct a mule-headed mathematician. They'd all need constant supervision. Maybe, she hoped, he wouldn't be able to find boots which fit. After all, she'd noticed he had big feet.

David watched as Carolyn drove off, a smile of satisfaction on his face. He knew that she didn't want him in the way. Turning, he walked into the house. In the basement, he could hear Ben's voice. He knew that he was putting in the piping between the house and the septic system. That thought brought David to a standstill. He realized that he was going to have to make some decisions about the bathrooms soon. Maybe he'd ask Ben. He'd know what to do.

David wandered into the battered old kitchen. The late afternoon sun brightened the room and accented the truly ugly floor. He closed his eyes and tried to imagine how the various woods he had seen would look. Why was it so hard to do? How come other people could imagine a room, choose the furniture and coordinate the colors and he couldn't? Carolyn was right. He was a concept person. He knew the idea of the room, but not the details. His mother should have made him work in the kitchen. Then, he'd have known what to do.

The unfairness of that thought made David squirm. Both his parents, and even his brother and sister, had recognized his unusual gifts and accommodated his needs. While his siblings had learned the fundamentals of cooking, he'd been allowed to work away at his computer.

David hated the sense of not knowing what was going to happen in the kitchen. He didn't like being out of control. Then, he had a brilliant idea. He'd wait. He'd tell Carolyn not to finish the room. Surely, when he met the woman who would make a suitable wife, he'd be able to ask her. After all, there would be no point in completing a kitchen that she'd dislike.

Pleased with the idea, David wandered on through the house. Then he remembered Cindy. She knew about kitchens; she was almost a chef. He'd clean up and return to the marina. Maybe he could talk her into having supper with him.

*       *       *

Carolyn stood looking out the kitchen window, lost in thought. Dusk was close at hand and the sun angled across the yard, touching the tulips and making them luminous. She could hear a mother calling her children. Bedtime was soon.

She realized she was fighting the impulse to go into the small building at the rear of their backyard. It was her space; a workshop where she practiced carpentry. In her spare time, she created models; models of the homes she hoped to construct some day. She knew that if she stepped out into the twilight and headed for her workshop, she was committed.

Carolyn walked into the living room and contemplated the television, but it was not going to satisfy her. With a sigh, she headed for the backyard.

Inside her workshop, she examined the model she'd already started of David's house. It was made so that the roof and second floor could be removed and she could look into the first- or second-floor rooms. Her fingers itched to complete it. Ideas crammed her head, fighting to get out. But it was the kitchen that was really on her mind.

She should make a model for David of the plan he'd suggested. Then, he'd find it easier to think about flooring and cupboards. It would be a marvelous kitchen, a cook's dream. The family room would be a warm and welcoming place to strew comics across the floor; a place to curl up with a book or to play a game of monopoly.

Well, why shouldn't she make a model of it? Having given in to the urge, she quickly assembled materials and sat down at her planning board.

## *Chapter Four*

David was ready before 7:00 the next morning. Figuring the work would be extremely dirty, he'd donned old jeans and a long-sleeved sweatshirt. While waiting for the work crew, he sat in one of the verandah chairs, admiring his new workboots. Tapping his feet together, he enjoyed the hard thud of their metal toes. He lifted the safety glasses from the table beside him and fitted them on. Donning his work gloves, he couldn't help the sense of satisfaction he felt knowing that Ms. Thompson would not be able to quibble about his equipment.

The sight of her van turning up the drive had him quickly pulling off the glasses and gloves. As he approached, the van doors opened and two tall, strong teenagers and an older man stepped out.

Carolyn went to the back of the van and proceeded to hand each person safety glasses, a mask and heavy work gloves. Turning to him, she said, "Hi, David. I'd like you to meet your workmates." Nodding toward a tall, red-headed teenager, she said, "This is Ted." A slightly shorter, dark, curly-headed young man was Philip. Then, she turned toward the older man. He was slightly stooped with a weary expression. "This is Hugo." David shook hands all around.

Carolyn said, "I see you're all fitted out. Here's a hard hat and mask." She proceeded to hand out hard hats to the others. Finally, she hauled out a plastic wheelbarrow where all the safety equipment and a number of tools were stored. Turning to the teenagers, she said, "Would you take this up to the second floor. Don't begin any work until I get there."

Memories of David's construction boss took over. *She'll probably boss us around all morning just like Linda did,* he thought, as he headed up the stairs after the others.

Arms folded across his chest, David leaned back against the cracked plaster wall and watched. Carolyn turned to the two boys. "Since this is the first time you've done this kind of work, I'm going to show you the routine." She handed each boy a crowbar. "Each of you will break the old plaster and lath from the walls, but only up to the line I've drawn. It's about a foot from the ceiling. Do not go any higher. Let me know if any piece breaks away and takes plaster above that line. David, you and Hugo will shovel the material into the wheelbarrow, then Hugo will wheel it to the window with the chute, and tip the stuff into the chute. If Hugo can keep up by himself, then you can help the boys."

Carolyn picked up an extra crowbar and bent down toward the bottom of the wall. She levered the crowbar into a broken edge of lath and began to pry it out. "Start at the bottom, boys, and work your way across. Each of you can work at a different wall. Remember. Do not tackle the ceiling yet."

As she continued to instruct the boys, David could not help but admire her. Why did she have to look so attractive, even when she was dressed like some space-age explorer with goggles and all? Then, he caught Ted looking at her as well. David snapped to attention, a frown on his face. Who the devil did the young pup think he was? The boy caught his expression and had the grace to blush.

Carolyn finished by saying, "Hugo, if you have time, try to use the broom to keep the mess down." Turning to the rest of them, she said, "I'll work with you for a few minutes just to see how you settle in."

For awhile, all David could hear was the chipping of plaster and screech of lath as it was pried off the wall studs. Behind the walls, he was surprised to find absolutely no insulation.

"They must have frozen in the winter," David observed. Carolyn nodded. "You ask any of the old-timers around here and they'll tell you about ice on the walls, and floors that were frigid. Getting up on a winter's morning was not a pleasant experience."

David had to admit that she was nothing like his exboss Linda. Carolyn made a point of praising each of them. She explained what to do when one of the them hit a difficult spot. Soon everyone was working as a team. The boys relaxed and began to chatter as they worked. Pleased with their progress, Carolyn left with instructions that they were to call her if there was a problem.

Once David settled in, he found he had time to think of other things. His trip to the marina the night before had been a success. He'd arrived about 6:00 and had been able to sit in the area Cindy was serving. When he was seated, Cindy greeted him and asked where Carolyn was. He'd been surprised by the question until he realized that Cindy had thought they were an item. He'd hastened to explain that Carolyn and her family were renovating his home. When his meal was finished, he'd asked Cindy when she was through with work. When she'd said that she was just about finished, he'd asked her to join him for coffee.

He'd found Cindy to be a very poised and confident young woman. They'd talked about everything except cooking. David decided to wait and strengthen their friendship before asking her for advice about his kitchen.

Carolyn worked downstairs while they removed the plaster. She'd carefully taken off the baseboard and any other trim upstairs during the week the house had been lifted. Each piece was numbered so that it could be put back into its original position unless, of course, it needed repair or replacement.

Now, she was removing the same items downstairs. It was a handy job to be doing since she wanted to be able to check on the two teenagers and especially on Hugo. He had recently lost his job in Stewart's Falls when a small furniture business closed. From everything she'd heard, he was a hardworking and dependable individual. They needed an extra workman so, at her father's suggestion, she had contacted him to work with the boys removing the plaster. If he worked out, they would hire him full-time while the project lasted. Hopefully, there would be another job right after so they could keep him on.

Carolyn was just numbering the last board in the living room when she heard a yell, a colossal thud, and a yelp of pain. Terrified, she was up the stairs before she was conscious of moving. She'd already guessed what had happened. Reaching the doorway, she saw exactly what she expected. A chunk of the ceiling had fallen.

As she entered the boys were lifting the plaster off David while Hugo knelt beside him. For a moment, she thought he was unconscious, as he had fallen backward. All she could see was his head and his legs, one sprawled out, the other bent. His hard hat had rolled in the corner and there was blood on his forehead. And then to her relief she saw him roll on his side and sit up. He coughed, then lifted his hand gingerly to his head.

Carolyn was beside him in a second. Kneeling, unable to control the wobble in her voice, she asked, "Are you alright?" Tentatively she touched David's face. Her hand was trembling so much that she hastily removed it.

Ruefully, David shrugged. "I think so." Looking at his fingers, he said, "I think I've cut myself."

Turning to the boys, Carolyn asked, "What exactly happened?"

They in turn looked confused. Before they could speak, Hugo explained. "We heard a crack and looked up to see the plaster separating from the ceiling. Ted stepped back to get out of the way, then tripped over the wheelbarrow and went head over heels. As he did, he knocked David's hat with his hand and sent it flying. A second later, the plaster descended. It caught David on the forehead. It just grazed him. I think he's alright."

Carolyn tried to breathe slowly and gain control. She eyed the ceiling. Another piece was hanging perilously. "We need to get out of here. Boys, take your lunch break. Now."

Turning back to David, she asked, "Do you think you're able to get up?" He proceeded to do so. Standing beside him, she instructed Hugo. "You take one arm, I'll take the other. We'll go over to the cabin. I'll get the first aid kit."

But David didn't want any of her coddling. He shook off her hand. "I'm quite capable of getting myself over to the cabin. I certainly don't need you playing nurse-maid."

Carolyn couldn't help but understand why he was angry. The ceiling should not have fallen. However, she had no intention of letting him go unattended. Not backing down, she said, "Walk over by yourself if you must, but Hugo will stay close by you. And I am definitely looking at that wound. I will also have to fill out an accident report."

She watched David walk across the grass to the cabin as she got the first aid kit from her van. She was relieved to see that he was steady on his feet. The plaster must have just glanced off him. Hugo walked beside him but made no effort to assist him. She was impressed with the calm way he'd handled things.

She wished she felt as composed. She'd never had an accident on-site before. Her father had taught them all to be very careful. She had personally checked the ceilings in the rooms herself and had been convinced they were stable. She had the men start on the walls first because she'd wanted them to have some experience before tackling the more difficult part of the job. She'd intended to work with them when they got to the ceilings. She'd have to figure out what had caused that particular piece of plaster to fall before they continued.

Hugo was coming out of the cabin door when she reached it. "Thanks, Hugo. You were a great help. Go and have your lunch now. I want to look at that ceiling before we start again. Make sure the guys don't go up there."

Carolyn didn't waste time knocking. Instead she marched right into the cabin, kit in hand. David was standing in front of a mirror he'd hung by the sink examining his head.

Carolyn grabbed a chair and dragged it over to the sink. "Please sit down, David. I want to clean that wound."

David was ready to argue but one glance at her white face made him realize that she was easily as shaken as he was. He couldn't help notice that her fingers trembled as she opened the first aid kit.

Sitting down, he watched her find his only basin and pour bottled water into it. From her first aid box she picked out a packaged antiseptic wipe and turned toward him nervously. He could see her eyeing his head with some trepidation.

Trying to ease her anxiety, he asked, "Aren't you going to warn me that this will hurt? They always do in the movies."

She looked at him askance, then realized he was teasing her. It was the last reaction she'd expected. He'd certainly been annoyed over at the house but now—he was joking? She'd expected him to tell her how incompetent she was to have a ceiling fall.

Squeezing his eyes shut like a little boy, he urged, "C'mon. Get it over with. I'll be brave."

Suddenly it didn't seem a simple task to wash the wound. She became very conscious that she had to touch him, to lean over him, and hold his head with her fingers as she daubed the antiseptic. Bracing herself, she gingerly placed her fingers on his head and tilted it away from her. Then she began to pat the dirt from the wound.

To her horror, she realized that the edge of the plaster had sliced the flesh along the right side of his forehead as well as scraping along his cheek. She grabbed another wipe and worked around the cut and along his cheek. For good measure, she daubed on antiseptic she knew burned.

During the entire time, he said not a word. After a few moments, he opened his eyes and watched her. His eyes weren't exactly grey, as she'd first thought. They had tiny spots of green around the iris while the outside was darkest charcoal. And they made her even more nervous. Gingerly, she pressed the cut together, trying to decide whether a butterfly bandage would keep the edges pressed together and whether the wound was really clean.

He reached up and gently pulled down her arm. "Carolyn, quit worrying. I took a good look at that slice. It's not deep enough for a stitch. Just put a few butterflies on it and cover it to keep it clean."

His touch rattled her even more. She was too aware of it. Hastily she busied herself opening a package of bandages. Then, taking a large breath to steady herself, she pulled the raw edges of the cut together and taped them. "I don't want you over in the dust again today. If you insist, you can work tomorrow."

When she saw his jaw clench stubbornly, she hurried on, "David, if you want to help, you can work with me downstairs. I just want you to stay out of that dust until a scab has formed on the deeper cut. I really could use the help. The boys and Hugo are quite capable of working by themselves and finishing the job."

Opening another package containing sterile cotton, she finished the job by washing the rest of his face with soap and cold water. She was so intent about doing everything right, so concerned about there being no infection that it took her a moment to realize that there was absolutely no reason on earth why he couldn't be doing this. Focusing on his face, she saw that he was sitting there with a perfectly ridiculous grin, watching her growing embarrassment as she realized what she was doing. She dropped the cloth into the basin as if it had singed her fingers and almost leapt away. "You can finish."

David smirked. He couldn't help himself. He'd enjoyed that little performance. Her touch had been soft and gentle. She'd been so serious, so completely unaware that she was close enough to swamp all his senses. In spite of the fact that she'd worked hard all morning, the scent of the wildflowers he'd smelled on her before washed over him. Her nearness, the sweet way she pursed her mouth, and her touch had been so unexpected.

The very idea of lusting after Carolyn Thompson brought him back to the real world. Briskly, he stood and took the basin and water. Moving to the mirror, he finished the task of cleaning up his face and hands. It didn't matter how cool it was today, he was going to have to wash in the lake. He shook his sweatshirt in an attempt to dislodge the plaster dust that had poured down his neck.

Feeling the need to reclaim his position as one who was uninterested and unaffected by her charms, he demanded, "Didn't you check the ceilings before we began work?"

Carolyn snapped her first aid kit shut. "Of course I did. I took the stepladder up there last week and tapped my way across all the rooms' ceilings and that of the hall. I have no idea why it came down. It's possible I'll never know. But I expect to discover as much as I can right now. That's if you're sure you're alright."

Ashamed of himself for taking his discomfort out on Carolyn, he said, "Go and get your lunch. We'll sit down here and relax. Afterwards, Hugo, you, and I will go and check the ceiling. And don't argue. I'm tall enough to help you. Hugo can hold the ladder while you examine it."

Carolyn wasn't sure she wanted to eat lunch with him. She'd been just a little too aware of him when she was cleaning his face. However, she was also too exhausted to fight. With a shrug, she muttered, "I'll go and get it."

As an afterthought, she asked, "When was your last tetanus shot?"

"Just last year. Quit worrying. I'm a big boy. Go get your lunch. I'm going to make a good strong pot of coffee."

After lunch, Carolyn hastily went back to the house to put away the trim she'd numbered. She was just about to go out the door when she heard a roar of laughter. Stepping out, she could see Ben and Mike and the rest of the crew standing around David. Because her brothers were so tall, she couldn't make out what the joke was at first, then Mike moved. To her amazement, she saw David in their midst, wearing a bright yellow shower cap pulled down to his eyebrows and covering the deeper cut. When he saw her, he called, "We're ready."

As they trooped past her into the house, he stopped. "Look, I've spoken to your brothers. It's not necessary to make an accident report. It would only upset your Dad."

Carolyn was about to argue but she knew he was right. Her father would start to worry that he'd put too much responsibility on her shoulders. The next thing that would happen would be that he'd be trying to do the work himself.

Quite overcome by David's observation of her father's condition and his thoughtfulness, she touched his arm. "Thank you. I think you're right about Dad."

Carolyn followed David upstairs to where Hugo and the boys were waiting.

Leading them into the room with the hanging plaster, she said, "I'd like to get this ceiling down so stand well back. Then you can finish the walls." Pulling a high step-ladder over to the gaping hole where some of the plaster still hung, Carolyn instructed. "First, I want to see if I can figure out why this ceiling came loose."

With that, she clamored up the ladder and examined the hole and the edge of the plaster. It made no sense. There was no reason why the ceiling had dropped that she could see. Looking down, she found that David was gripping the ladder. She couldn't help but chuckle. "David, you don't have to hold the ladder. It's very steady. Please, would you hand me a crowbar?"

Amused, Carolyn watched David look around for the tool while still holding the ladder. Just as quickly, Hugo handed it to him and he passed it on to her. "Watch out," she instructed and reached out toward the studs, lath, and plaster. Just as she was about to touch the materials, she felt a hand grip her ankle. Startled, she almost lost her balance.

"What in the . . ." Looking down, she saw David grimly holding her ankle. "For crying out loud, David," she exclaimed, "You nearly made me lose my footing."

Ignoring her when she tried to wiggle her foot, he growled, "Go ahead and reach over there or get down and let me move the ladder closer. I'm not letting anyone else get hurt in my house."

Carolyn couldn't believe her ears. *He* was telling *her* what to do. Glancing down, she saw him glaring mulishly from under the stupid yellow shower cap topped by his safety helmet. Deciding that having a fight at the top of a ladder was not too clever, she called, "Watch out," and jammed the crowbar between the lath and plaster. Another great portion came crashing down beside the ladder. Ignoring the hand on her ankle, she continued to work until her temper cooled. When it became necessary for her to move the ladder, she descended ready for a fight but David anticipated her and left the room with the wheelbarrow the boys had been filling. Hugo looked at her and grinned. The boys had the good sense to pretend they were busy.

Aggravated at them all, she hauled the ladder over so she could finish one side of the ceiling, then headed up the ladder ready to haul more plaster down. The second she leaned out, a hand gripped her ankle. Without looking down, she said between gritted teeth, "David, if you don't let go of me immediately, I'll refuse to let you work."

His hand only gripped her ankle harder. "Carolyn," he mimicked. "If you want to complete this renovation, then you will let me hold your ankle."

Looking down, and hefting her crowbar experimentally in her hand, she defied him. "You can't fire me. You signed a contract."

A nasty smile crossed David's face. "I'll tell your father about the accident."

He had her there and she knew it. "I hope the whole blasted ceiling falls on your smart-aleck face," she said, and began to tear plaster and lath off with a vengeance.

* * *

Driving the ball across the net, Carolyn waited, ready for Dan to return it. Purposely, Dan slowed the game by lobbing it into a corner. Carolyn steamed toward it and drove it back, sending Dan flying to the other side. He missed.

"That's it. Do you want another game?" asked Carolyn.

Wiping his forehead with his arm, Dan grimaced. "Not a chance. You hammered the daylights out of the ball, the racket, and me. Let's go across the street and get a cool drink and you can tell me just what is behind your desire to knock my head off."

When they were settled in the coffee shop, Dan said, "Okay. What's up?"

Carolyn rolled her eyes. "You won't believe the day I've had. First, the plaster fell from the ceiling we were working on and landed on David Reid."

Dan whistled. "Was he hurt?"

"Yes. He had a cut on the side of his head and a scratch on his cheek."

Dan considered what she had just said. "First question. How come his head was hurt if he had on a safety hat?"

Carolyn sighed. "Just rotten luck. The ceiling cracked and one of the boys stepped back to get out of the way. He fell into the wheelbarrow, and in doing so, his arm or hand, I don't know which, knocked David's hat off just as the plaster came down."

Dan couldn't help but grin as he imagined the boy falling into the wheelbarrow. Carolyn was indignant. "It's not funny. Someone could have been seriously hurt."

Reaching over, Dan patted her hand. "I know. Take it easy. No one was hurt. Relax. You were playing tennis as if all the demons in hell were after you. C'mon, Caro. You usually take everything in your stride. What's so different today?"

Taking a large gulp of her iced tea, Carolyn said, "You haven't heard anything yet."

She took another gulp and tried to contain her indignation. "When I went up the ladder to check the ceiling and pry off the rest of the plaster, David insisted on holding my ankle."

That was too much for Dan. He burst out laughing. "He did what?"

"He held my ankle." She glowered at him. "Quit laughing. Can you imagine trying to operate on a . . . a horse with someone clamped on to your arm?"

Dan settled back and tried to contain his amusement. He'd never seen Carolyn so worked up. Her eyes absolutely sparked, her cheeks flushed with annoyance. "Why didn't you tell him to clear out?"

"Believe me, I tried. And when he refused, I said he could no longer help. Then, he had the nerve to say if that was the case, I couldn't finish the renovations. I said he couldn't fire me, I had a contract. Then the rat had the nerve to say he would tell my father about the accident."

Dan couldn't resist asking, "And just where were you when this argument took place?"

"I was up the ladder and he was holding my ankle and, under his safety helmet, he was wearing a stupid yellow shower cap pulled down to his eyebrows."

That did it for Dan. He leaned back and howled. "A yellow shower cap?"

Really upset now that she was getting no sympathy, Carolyn muttered, "He wore that to keep the dust out of the cut on his head."

Standing, Dan held out his hand. "C'mon Caro. I'll walk you home and you can tell me just how you intend to get the rest of the plaster off the ceilings without first killing David Reid."

David, strolling up the street after a late supper, saw Carolyn leave the coffee shop in the company of her tennis partner. His arm was around her shoulder and he seemed to be consoling her.

It didn't take much imagination to figure out what they were talking about. He was sure he figured in the conversation as a first-rate jerk. David couldn't explain it himself. The sight of Carolyn at the top of that ladder had made him feel nauseous. Just because he was a first-rate coward when it came to climbing anything higher than three steps didn't mean other people couldn't do it safely. And yet, the minute she leaned over from the ladder, his heart had dropped like a stone. He'd felt like he was about to hyperventilate.

They'd argued all afternoon. Finally, Hugo came up with a solution. He would go up the ladder the next day. As he'd explained, he was as nimble as a goat and as strong as a horse. He'd get the job done while David loaded the plaster and took it to the chutes. The boys would work on the walls. Carolyn could finish the woodwork downstairs.

It had seemed like a good solution until Carolyn asked the obvious question. "How come it's alright for Hugo to go up a ladder and risk his neck?"

David hadn't been able to explain. In fact, he'd been embarrassed when no obvious reply came to mind.

David fastened his attention on Carolyn's disappearing figure. Wouldn't you know she'd have legs to die for, he thought bitterly. And she had no business wearing a little white tennis skirt. No one who wore workboots should be allowed to. Well, at least he'd won one battle. She would not be up the blasted ladder tomorrow.

Carolyn wandered around the house, recalling that her father was out playing euchre and relieved that she didn't have to fib to him about her day. Indignation still bubbled through her whenever she thought about the day's events. All her frustration was focused on the antics of David Reid. How was she going to get him out of her hair? She should never have agreed to his working with them.

She hunched her shoulders to ease the tension in them, all of which was caused by her employer. Knowing that she should try to unwind, she headed for her bedroom and en suite bathroom to soak and relax. But immersing herself in aromatic bath oil did nothing to calm her spirits. Having David hovering around her like an overprotective fairy godmother shook her confidence. No one had questioned her actions in years.

Giving up on the bath, she showered and shampooed her hair. In the bedroom, she settled down to the serious business of blow-drying her hair. Usually this had a calming effect, but tonight, she found herself still thinking about David, and with each stroke, returning to her earlier state of tension.

To make matters worse, she recalled the episode in the cabin when she'd cared for his wound. It didn't make her happy to admit that she'd been all too aware of him, of the feel of his skull under her fingertips or the way his smile tilted as he teased her.

He'd really surprised her. James would have had a fit if he'd been knocked on the head by a sheet of plaster. She knew he would have moaned and groaned and made a major fuss over the incident. He certainly would never have suggested that she forget the incident over consideration for her father. James's sense of his own importance had been far too strong. He probably would have insisted upon litigation immediately. But then, James would never have spent the day removing lath and plaster.

As Carolyn loosely braided her hair, she pondered the fact that David Reid was nothing like James. She wondered why she had ever thought he was. Then she recalled his attitude when she had first met him. His arrogance on that occasion had misled her. Oh, David was stubborn, and certainly annoying but on the other hand, he'd moved to the cabin without too much fuss. If only he wouldn't bug her on ladders.

Picking up a new sci-fi paperback, she settled down to read. She'd worry about David in the morning.


Carolyn nearly made it through the next day without incident. Hugo's idea had worked well and kept David upstairs fully occupied. Oh, he'd come downstairs to check on her occasionally but she kept her ears peeled, and the minute she heard anyone on the stairs she made sure she was numbering boards, far away from the short stepladder she needed to reach the top of doors and the windows.

By 4:00 she was nearly ready to call it quits but decided to take down the antique copper chandelier from the center of the dining room first. The ladder was short but sturdy, quite strong enough to hold her. She filled her tool pouch with the screwdrivers and pliers she would need and, checking the ladder for stability, started up with a delicious sense that she was getting away with murder.

The screws were difficult to budge. Deciding she needed a different tool, she began to back down. Two strong hands gripped her by the waist. The next thing she knew, she was suspended in the air, gaping like a fish out of water and then, spun around. Before she could figure out what had happened, she was caught and brought nose-to-nose with her employer, her feet still hanging.

He squinted his eyes at her and said in an unnaturally level voice. "What did I say about ladders, Carolyn?"

That did it. She aimed a kick guaranteed to make him let go of her, but he was too fast. He dropped her without warning so that she had to grab the side of the ladder to keep her balance.

Where had he come from and how in the earth had he managed to spin her in the air? She was almost as tall as he was and certainly weighed too much to be spun like that.

Moving the ladder out of the way, she shoved her face into his, so close she could see the pores in his skin and the scratches on his cheek. She could smell him, all plaster dust and perspiration. Unable to stop herself, she yelled, "Just what do you think you're doing? I put up with you yesterday bossing everyone around but I don't intend to do it anymore. You touch me one more time on that ladder and I'll sue you for harassment."

"Try it," he challenged.

"You don't think I will?"

"I think when you cool down, you'll see that it isn't in your best interest to make false charges against a client." He smiled meanly, "And your father would not like it either."

Beside herself with rage, she began to thump him on the chest with her index finger, stressing every point.

"Trust an arrogant academic to stoop to blackmail. You haven't got one reason why I should stay off that ladder so you have to threaten me. Take the fixture down yourself. I absolutely forbid anyone else to do it. Is that clear?"

Grabbing her toolbox, she stomped her way to the door, then turned. "And don't expect anyone here until next Tuesday." Walking to the bottom of the stairs, she yelled, "Hugo, guys, put your tools down. It's time to quit."

Ted leaned over the railing, "It's only just after four."

"That's alright," exclaimed Carolyn. "It's a holiday weekend. Have a good time. I'll see you at seven, Tuesday morning."

With that, she turned and walked out of the house, still muttering to herself when she reached the van. Heaving her tools in the back, she slammed the door as hard as she could, started the van, and spun the wheels as she left the yard.

David watched the others hurry down the stairs. Only Hugo stopped to say good-bye. And then they were all gone. The house was silent.

Suddenly very conscious that he had again lost his cool, he wandered outside to the verandah. Carolyn Thompson made him crazy. One look at her leaning out from the ladder to reach the light fixture and he was mindlessly grabbing her.

Then, for a moment, he grinned smugly, remembering the neat way he tossed her in the air. Took the wind right out of her sails. For about one second. With that kick she'd aimed at him, she'd intended to maim.

He still zinged from the rush he got from their confrontation. He could still feel her ribs expand as he gripped her waist, and see the widening of her eyes as he caught her. For one incredible moment, he'd had the overpowering urge to kiss her. Then sanity returned. Kiss Carolyn Thompson? Not likely. The very thought had had him dropping her like a hot potato.

He sat for awhile, his feet on the verandah railing, searching for the peace and quiet he had treasured just a few weeks before. Instead, he was aware of a sense of restlessness. Suddenly, the place was too quiet. Sure, the birds were busy singing and Carolyn's orioles were whistling but suddenly he was aware that he missed the companionship of the boys and Hugo. Of course, he assured himself, he did not miss Carolyn.

A purred call announced Charlie as he leaped up on the verandah railing and performed a delicate tightrope walk along its edge. "No mouse?" David demanded.

Charlie jumped into his lap and up onto his shoulder. Purrs and plaintive cries told about his busy day. But for once, Charlie's companionship was not enough. Heading for the cabin, David called, "C'mon, Charlie. Come and talk to me while I freshen up. Think I'll go over to the marina for supper. I might find Cindy."

Charlie followed, chasing a butterfly and attacking a wildflower moving in the breeze. At the cabin door, David invited him in. As he fed the cat, he thought, I'll just throw my tennis gear in the trunk in case Cindy's busy.

## *Chapter Five*

Feeling slightly out of sorts, David drove back to Stewart's Falls. He might as well have saved himself a trip to the marina. It had been so busy that Cindy barely had time to say hello. He'd forgotten about the beginning of the holiday weekend when southern Ontarians worked in their gardens or traveled out of the cities to their cottages. Victoria Day could not have come at a better time for a population tired of winter and anxious to enjoy the warmth of spring.

David headed for the tennis courts. Parking behind the small clubhouse, he saw that all three courts were busy. He recognized some of the group waiting for a turn, Ben and Barbara among them. As he hurried in to change, he thought, this may be my chance to get to know Barbara better.

Carolyn and Dan walked up the street toward the courts. Dan was still chuckling at the latest installment in what he jokingly called "The Battle of the Ladder." Carolyn was scowling. "C'mon," coaxed Dan. "It's a holiday. You have three whole days to forget about David."

Carolyn turned to him. "You're right. I won't have to look at his smarmy, interfering face until Tuesday." With that she increased her pace. Waving her racket at Dan as he trailed behind, she called, "Hurry up."

Dan watched her with appreciation and regret. She walked with confidence, her pleated white tennis skirt and long legs enough to raise the temperature of any male. But attraction had not been enough for either of them. He could no more fathom why he couldn't fall in love with her any more than Carolyn could figure out why she was not in love with him. She would have made an ideal veterinarian's wife since her own busy schedule would help her understand his erratic hours as a country vet. Still, she was a good friend and he should stop teasing her about her temperamental employer.

They met Ben and Barbara in time to sense that they had had some kind of disagreement. Maybe, Carolyn thought, Ben's teasing had gone just a little too far. Why he couldn't admit to himself that it was Barbara he wanted mystified her. It was obvious to everyone else.

The foursome on the court were just finishing their last set when Carolyn heard Ben call, "Hi, David. You're going to have to wait for a court."

She heard him reply, "No trouble." Carolyn took a long slow breath to calm her resentment. Was there no place to get away from him? He'd probably be running up to catch her if she leaped high to slam a ball.

Just as they were taking their rackets from their presses, Dan's pager beeped. Checking it, he moved a distance away and made a telephone call. With a look of regret, he returned to the group. "I'm sorry, Carolyn. I've got to go. Farmer has a sick cow."

Before she could say a word, Barbara piped up. "Don't worry. David can play with me and Ben can play with Carolyn. Okay?" she asked brightly.

"Fine with me," David replied. "Always happy to help a damsel in distress."

Distress, my foot, Carolyn thought. Barbara was just giving Ben a hard time. And from the look of it, Ben knew it. Scowling, he spun his racket and muttered, "Great."

If David caught the undertones, he ignored them.

For the first few rallies, the four of them tested each other out both as partners and opponents. It was not until Carolyn found herself serving to David that her attitude to the game changed.

As she raised her racket to serve, she found herself focusing on his face, and all the resentment and frustration she'd suffered because of him exploded in her serve. It blistered the air as she drove it inches inside the baseline, but out of his reach. A surge of victory pumped through her as she saw his look of surprise.

She moved to serve to Barbara. She drove a serve across that any reasonable player could return and Barbara did just that. The rally continued for a few moments before Carolyn sent the ball flying to a corner on her left.

Again she was facing David, but this time he was watching her warily, knees bent, bouncing gently from side to side. As before, an inexplicable surge of feeling raced through her and she slammed the ball in the back corner. This time, he caught it and returned it with equal power, tossing it toward Ben who returned it to Barbara. The rally continued until Ben managed to drop a ball right over their net.

They played two sets. More and more, Carolyn became aware that she and David were monopolizing the action, and that it was becoming quite heated. Finally, at the end of the second game, Ben threw his racket in the air, caught it and said, "Look, you two. You might as well have it out in a singles match." Jumping over the net, he grabbed Barbara's hand. "C'mon, Barb. Let's go and have a cool drink across the street. I want to talk to you anyway."

David found himself torn between a feeling of vexation that Ben had neatly snatched Barbara away and a rush of exhilaration at the thought of facing-off with Carolyn. When he saw the look of consternation cross her face as those watching heckled for the match, he couldn't help a satisfied grin. It was that smug smirk that committed Carolyn.

A small crowd had gathered. Someone jumped out and tossed a coin. Carolyn called it and won first serve.

"Three sets, David?" she challenged.

Going back to the line, David took a ready stance. "Three sets it is."

Carolyn slammed her first serve straight at his feet but he lightly side-stepped and drove it into the other court. She was there in time to set it beautifully just over the net. He missed.

Their audience cheered. "Fifteen love."

Very pleased with herself, Carolyn decided to change her tactics and drove her serve to the upper edge of the court, but he anticipated her. He caught the serve and slowed it down so it dribbled over the net out of her reach.

"Way to go," yelled their audience. "Fifteen all."

Excitement continued to surge through Carolyn. She tapped the ball for a few moments, considering her next move. Eyeing David, she saw that he was back at the baseline, rocking gently from side to side, waiting, with a look of concentration that unnerved her for a moment.

Choosing action to help her focus, she sent a service blurring by him but it was outside the baseline. Serving again, Carolyn sent a hard fast drive to his left. He did the impossible. He reached with his left hand and lobbed it over the net.

Dashing forward, she slammed it down and he lifted it up and over her head to drop it neatly just inside the baseline.

"Great move," someone from the sidelines called and David grinned. "Fifteen-Thirty."

Determined now to even the score, Carolyn sent a slow straight serve right at him, just coaxing him to slam it but he twisted and sent it to the right. Just in time she caught it and returned it. He tried to drop it over the net but she caught it and sent it over his head. He missed.

The crowd yelled "Thirty all."

She waited a moment, watching David watching her as she rocked gently, twirling her racket, stretching out the suspense. Then, with onc swift movement, she slammed the ball into the far edge of the court. He missed. It was her turn to grin with satisfaction.

The crowd whistled and kept score. "Forty-Thirty."

Her next serve was not so successful. He caught it and slammed into the far corner. "Deuce."

Three times they reached deuce, each playing as hard as they could. In the end, David managed two scores in a row and won the game and eventually, the set.

By then both of them were hot and tired, and out of breath. Going over to the benches to drink some bottled water, David called, "Had enough?"

Carolyn looked at him surprised. "You want to quit?"

"Not a chance."

Gulping down some water, Carolyn wiped her face with the back of her arm. "Ready anytime you are."

David watched her saunter back to the court. He knew that she couldn't be as cool as she pretended. He was absolutely winded. He hadn't had a game like this since he'd taken to the country in March.

She took a pose of sheer provocation. Crossing one foot over the other, she leaned on her tennis racket, as if she hadn't a care in the world. The audience loved it.

Striding out to the court, David tried to appear as nonchalant as his aching muscles would let him. Taking a moment, he straightened his headband in an effort to clear the perspiration from his forehead.

"Maybe you need your yellow shower cap," he heard her call sweetly.

That did it. A surge of pure annoyance washed over him. She wanted to make fun of him, did she? Well, he'd show her. Throwing the ball in the air, he served it with unerring accuracy to the one place she couldn't reach. When she'd recovered, he called, "Not bad for an arrogant academic, eh?"

"Touché."

The play continued; Carolyn slamming out her frustrations, still burning from his high-handedness over the ladder and David, knowing what drove her, openly challenging her. The crowd was enchanted, sensing that there was more than just a tennis match at stake. Finally, it came to the last game. The crowd had grown, some cheering for Carolyn, others supporting David.

David had the serve. This time, he made her wait, bouncing the ball on the ground, more to get his breath than to aggravate her. He wanted this game over before he collapsed. She, on the other hand, looked poised, ready for anything he could offer. He had to admit to himself that it was the most exciting game he'd ever played.

Buoyed by the thought, he sent a serve blistering toward her. She returned it backhand. He drove it back and forced her to the baseline. She returned his shot to the corner and moved up to correctly anticipate his next shot. He couldn't stop the motion he'd planned. To his chagrin he watched the ball move toward her, just begging to be slammed back. She didn't disappoint him. The audience whistled, stamped their feet and yelled, "Love-Fifteen."

David watched Carolyn for a moment; she was standing ready, shifting her racket from hand to hand. A skein of hair had escaped and tumbled over her shoulder. As he sent his serve across the net, he realized he'd lost his focus. She easily returned it out of his reach.

Catcalls and whistles brought him back to his senses. He had no intention of losing a game just because he was distracted by a pretty girl. If he had to lose, it would be because he'd played a good game, but she'd played better.

Shaking his head, David brought his energies to the game and for the next long rally, kept his eye right on the ball. It was a good rally, exhilarating, challenging, and in the end, he got the point, Thirty-Fifteen.

Although his lungs were bursting from the effort, he sent another ball steaming into the far corner. She made a frantic plunge with her left hand and missed.

This time the men in the crowd were yelling encouragement and calling the score. "Thirty all."

Looking across at her, he saw the challenge in her eyes and his exhaustion vanished. Readying for the serve, he sent it to her left. She lifted it back to his right even as he moved to center. Throwing himself through the air, he caught the ball and sliced it sideways. He scored. "Forty-Thirty."

Needing a moment to get his breath, he knelt and retied his running shoes, much to the amusement of the onlookers. He was too tired to care. Carolyn walked up and down the baseline, heaving exaggerated sighs and switching her racket back and forth. Again the crowd loved her nonsense.

Taking his position to serve, David carefully considered his next shot. With care, he could end the game. He'd noticed that Carolyn was faster to the right than the left so he sent a ball to the left front just behind the line. She caught it and sent it whizzing past him. Deuce!

He tried again, same place, but she wasn't fooled. She caught it and sent it angling over the net to the other side just out of his reach.

David wiped his forehead with his arm. One more return like that and she'd have the game. The noise from the audience was getting louder, threatening his concentration. He bounced the ball and planned. He sent one down the baseline, nicely placed, and she sent it back. Swooping it up with his racket he cleverly arced it just above her head hoping that she wouldn't be able to return it.

And then it happened. His contractor without her heavy workboots seemed to levitate in the air, her body bent in an exquisite arc, her racket just touching the ball to tip it over the net. In desperation, he scooped it up and sent it sailing right out of the court.

The game was hers.

Pandemonium broke out. Cheers and clapping urged them on to a third set. Suddenly David realized that he didn't want to continue play. He didn't want one of them better than the other. Not tonight, anyway.

The cheering and good-natured heckling continued as he walked up to the net. Seeing his approach, Carolyn met him on the other side. "You still mad?" he asked.

His question caught her off guard, but after a moment's hesitation, she said, "No."

"Then let's call it a day. You played a magnificent game. I, on the other hand, am absolutely wiped out. I'll be lucky to make it to the coffee shop." He paused for a moment to see if she'd object, to see whether it was important for her to prove that she was the best. When she didn't say anything, he continued, "Quite frankly, I don't care if we ever prove one of us is better than the other. I just like playing with you."

That brought a smile to her face. But before she could say anything, he stunned himself by reaching out and lifting a long tendril of hair that had caught on her damp cheek. Gently, he tucked it behind her ear.

Quite startled by his action, her eyes widened, and for a moment, there only seemed to be the two of them on the court, caught in some strange wordless exchange. Hastily she stepped back and he hurriedly moved off the court.

"Play-off," the crowd chanted, but David just shook his head.

"A draw. The court is yours."

Packing up his gear, David went over to Carolyn and said, "Let's go and get a cool drink. My treat."

Carolyn stood at the kitchen sink and filled the coffee pot. Turning off the water, she remained there, staring out the window lost in thought. She should be exhausted today but wasn't. Instead she'd wakened early, full of energy, unable to stay in bed another minute.

What a game they'd had last night. She hadn't been

challenged like that by anyone, not even Dan. She frowned. She couldn't quite understand, yet, why David decided not to play the third set. He'd admitted that he was wiped out but she was sure that hadn't been the reason. Oddly enough, he seemed to like the fact that there had been no winner. He'd said the same again over the cool drinks they had at the coffee shop.

He was a strange man, she thought. Just when she thought she'd figured him out, was sure she had him pigeonholed, he'd do something completely unexpected.

Why was his desire not to have a winner so unexpected? she asked herself. And then the truth dawned. She was still judging David on the basis of James's behavior. He'd have played until he won. And if he'd lost he would have stomped off in a foul mood. Thinking about it now, Carolyn wondered how she could have been such a fool, getting all dewy-eyed over such a pretentious and self-centered jerk.

She returned to her task and finished preparing the coffeemaker. As she turned it on, the image of David formed in her mind, his long-legged body arched in the air, his arm outstretched for the ball, ready to slam it across the net. She simply couldn't stop the thought. He was gorgeous. He moved with a sinuous grace on the court, pivoting and reaching, seemingly without effort, although she knew that it had been. He'd admitted as much, said that he'd spent two months hunched over his computer with only the occasional jog as the winter eased off and the roads cleared.

She began to prepare her breakfast, putting water in a pan, dropping in an egg to poach, and placing bread in the toaster. Then, she remembered something else. She recalled as he'd walked her back to her house the night before how he'd hemmed and hawed, and finally said that he didn't want to make decisions about his kitchen. He'd leave that part of the renovation for last. When she pointed out that it would hold up the wiring and plumbing and make the job more expensive, he just shrugged. He reminded her that money was no object. Anyway, he'd added, he thought the woman who was to live in the house should have the final say. He'd wait until he found a wife.

Carolyn chuckled. Wait until he found a wife! Shaking her head at the naïveté of the whole idea, she mused about the peculiar combination of characteristics that made up David Reid; idealistic about finding a wife, stubborn when he made up his mind about something, thoughtful on more than one occasion, and absolutely bullheaded at other times.

He'd surprised her, however, by making two quite sensible decisions. He announced that he wanted flooring in the kitchen that would match the rest of the house— a decision she agreed with completely. Then, to her amazement, he went on to discuss the windows. He had, he said, been driving around, looking at other houses of the same vintage. All of them seemed to have the same type of window unless the house had been renovated. He wanted to have windows made to match the originals. The windows he had in mind were double-hung with only two panes of glass in each unit. Upon reflection, she agreed with him. He was absolutely right. The popular habit of replacing the windows with multi-paned glass might be fashionable but not true to the house.

Just as Carolyn was carrying her breakfast to the table, she heard the clatter of her brother's feet coming down the stairs. It was a family joke that Ben found it impossible to walk down anything quietly.

As she sat down to eat, he bounced into the kitchen

and leaned over to give her a quick peck. "Good morning, Caro. Great day, isn't it? How come you're up so early?"

Carolyn could quite easily have asked the same of him. Ben was notorious for hating the morning, needing four alarm clocks to wake him, and always being grumpy until he had coffee. Even stranger, here he was, giving her a brotherly peck.

He hummed his way over to the counter to pour himself coffee and returned to the table, dancing to the tune.

Not only was Ben bouncing with energy, he was dressed in his casual, but in this case, elegant best. No grubby jeans or atrocious T-shirt. Instead he wore a crisp blue cotton shirt and chinos. No runners. Shining brown loafers graced his feet.

Sitting down, he snatched one of her pieces of toast.

Carolyn grabbed at it and missed. "Go and put some more bread in the toaster."

He spun out of his seat, cha-chaed over to the toaster, her piece still in his hand, put more bread in and cha-chaed back. Grinning away, still very pleased with himself, he lathered marmalade all over the toast, then crunched into the slice.

Carolyn ate her breakfast and waited. Something was up. Ben and she were very close. Her mother had died when she was fifteen and Ben eighteen, and he had taken his role of older brother seriously, watching out for her, giving unwanted advice, and supervising her dates. Even in adulthood, they were close.

She waited as he consumed all the extra toast and another cup of coffee. He took his dishes to the dishwasher and then, with his back to her, said, "Hmm, Caro, what are you doing this morning now that you're up so early?"

She didn't know herself, so she said, "Nothing in particular. Why?"

Still with his back to her, he said, "Well, I wondered if you'd have time to give my hair a trim."

Carolyn nearly blew her coffee across the breakfast table. Ben was famous for letting his blond curls dust his shoulders before allowing anyone near him with a pair of scissors. As far as she could see, he was only halfway to another cut.

She waited until he turned around when she made no answer, curious to see his face. However, all he did was raise his eyebrows, waiting for an answer.

Giving in, knowing that he'd tell her what he was up to when he was ready, she shrugged. "Sure, I have time. Get the scissors and clippers."

They both knew the routine by heart. Ben got a stool, the cutting equipment, and an old tablecloth kept just for the occasion. Carolyn got an old towel.

Spreading the tablecloth on the kitchen floor, Ben put the stool in the center and sat on it. Carolyn handed him a towel which he wrapped securely around himself, protecting his clean blue shirt.

"The usual?" she asked as she got the scissors out of the package. There was a pause, and then he said, "Uh, maybe just a little bit shorter."

Really curious now, Carolyn began to snip. She'd been cutting Ben's hair since their mother died. Although she was no professional, she still thought she did a fair job. However, Ben had always resisted her desire to give him a really classy cut. He had gorgeous hair, thick, springy, and curly and she'd been dying to style it for ages. At last, she was to get her chance.

As she snipped, Ben said, "Hear you had quite a pair

of sets last night. How come you didn't play the rest of them?"

Carolyn continued her snipping. "We decided before we started that we were only going to play three sets. There were a half dozen people waiting for the courts."

"Yes, but I understand that you didn't play the third set. That it was a draw. How come? It's not like you. I'd have thought you would've welcomed a chance to slam a few at David Reid. After all, he's been driving you nuts at work. Hauling you off ladders and being a regular nuisance."

Carolyn peered around his shoulder to look into his innocent blue eyes. "Oh? And just who told you that?"

"C'mon, Carolyn," he grinned. "Don't be stupid. Those kids you have working couldn't wait to tell me how he kept holding onto your foot. I guess he learned last night that you weren't as helpless as he seemed to think."

"Actually," she admitted, "he is the best player I've ever had a game with. He played fair and square. I'm not sure which one of us would have won the final set. He said he'd rather wait and have another go some other time."

Ben settled back while Carolyn continued to cut until she had one side done and then she stopped. Ben was not the only one who could tease. She took a stance before him, folded her arms and said, "Now, brother dear, if you want to leave here with the two sides of your head even, you'll 'fess up. Just what is all this about?"

Ben tried to play dense. "What do you mean, 'all of this'?"

"I mean good blue shirt and chinos, polished loafers, and a smart haircut."

Ben actually blushed and then he looked right at her.

His eyes glittered with satisfaction when he said, "Barbara is looking for a new car and I offered to help. We're going to spend the day in Smithboro shopping."

Not daring to say the wrong thing, Carolyn went back to snipping before she replied, "That's very nice of you, Ben."

He snorted. "You don't have to sound so smug about it. I know you think Barb is a nice girl. Just right for me."

Carolyn peered around at him again. "When have I ever said that?"

"Oh, it wasn't so much what you said as how you watched the two of us."

"You're crazy, big brother." Then to change the subject, "What brought on all this interest in helping Barb choose a car?"

She was brushing off the loose hair on his shoulders while she waited for his answer. Finally, he muttered, "I didn't like the way your David Reid was hustling her."

It was Carolyn's turn to sputter. "He's not *my* David Reid. And when did he ever hustle her?"

"Well, he couldn't partner with her fast enough last night."

Carolyn grinned. "As far as I can recall, it was Barbara who grabbed David's hand and claimed him as her partner."

He scowled. "Well, it doesn't matter. We had a talk and . . .", there was a pause. "Well, I think I might like to see more of her."

Carolyn couldn't help but smile broadly. "Well, good luck, big brother. Happy hustling."

He turned on her at that. "I'm not hustling, Caro, and don't you ever say to anyone that I am." He reddened again. "I'm er-r, . . . ." he hunted for the right word. "I'm courting her."

She couldn't help but laugh at his outdated word and his expression. He grabbed the towel from his shoulder and threatened to shake it all over her if she didn't stop. She was saved when her father entered the kitchen. "I can't believe you're both up on a holiday weekend. By the way, Ben, I wondered if you could help me get some flowers for the beds around the house today?"

Carolyn caught Ben's look of consternation. Both of them tried to save their dad when they could. "I'll do it," Carolyn said. Over her dad's shoulders, she mouthed, "You owe me."

The two of them tidied up the kitchen as their father made his breakfast. "Oh, by the way, Carolyn," Ben said, "I asked David to the barbecue on Monday."

She couldn't believe her ears. "You did what?"

"Asked him to the barbecue." And then with a grin, he added, "Mind you, I suggest that you hide any ladders before he arrives."

In all innocence, their father asked, "What's this about ladders?"

Before Carolyn could stop him, Ben said, "It seems that David Reid cannot stand to see Carolyn climb a ladder. Whenever she goes up one, he holds her foot for fear she'll lose her balance. He seems to have some sort of ladder fetish or . . .", he said grinning, "Maybe it's a foot fetish."

With that, he dodged out of the kitchen before she could retaliate.

David approached the Thompson house with some trepidation. True, Ben had asked him to the barbecue but what if he hadn't mentioned it to his dad, or more important, to Carolyn? After all, except for the tennis match, they hadn't exactly hit it off. After the episodes with the ladders, he thought it was possible that she'd prefer a break from him.

As he reached the house, he could hear laughter from the backyard. He paused for a moment, and then gave himself a silent lecture. It wasn't as if he were shy. His belief in himself and his enthusiasm for what he did gave him the confidence to handle most situations. Squaring his shoulders, he walked up the path beside the house.

He stopped and watched the activity. Up on a large deck he could see Jim Thompson and Andy talking while they watched Mike and a tiny woman with short blond hair, who David guessed was his wife, playing croquet with their two children in addition to Ben and Barbara. From the sounds of it, the game was a lot of fun. There was laughter and advice laced with encouragement. He watched as Mike helped the youngest child, a little girl, swing her mallet.

They reminded him of his own family who, he knew, would be busy at their nursery all day. It might be a national holiday, but not for people selling bedding plants. This was the first weekend when it was considered warm enough to plant annuals.

Looking around again, he realized that he could not see Carolyn.

Andy saw him first and came over. "Glad you could come, David. Come along and I'll introduce you to Mike's family. I think you know everybody else."

After meeting Mike's wife, Naomi, and their children, ten-year-old Lynn and twelve-year-old Peter, he found himself drawn into another game of croquet along with Andy.

From then on, the afternoon was a pleasant blur. Two

games later, Carolyn, in a blue T-shirt and shorts, joined them along with her dad. The large yard, with its tall old oaks and maples, rang with their laughter. And if David was aware that Carolyn made sure she played on the other side, he didn't let it bother him. At least there were no ladders around for him to make a fool of himself.

Everyone helped with supper. Everyone, that is, except Carolyn. David was surprised when her brothers shooed her away from the barbecue. Ben explained. "Carolyn spent all of yesterday buying annuals and planting them. Too often she gets stuck with more than her share. Anyway, I think Peter wants to talk to her." And as David watched, Carolyn and her nephew disappeared inside.

Andy barbecued. David and Ben arranged two picnic tables end-to-end on the deck and then were given the task of setting them by Naomi who instructed that they were to make them "really nice."

Ben made this a game. Every time he led David into the kitchen, he challenged him. "Okay, what else do we need to make the tables *real nice*?" Entering into the spirit of the game, they managed to go through the kitchen drawers and find tablecloths and napkins.

"You know who is going to have to launder these when we're finished," Ben grumbled. "But it'll be worth it to get Naomi's goat."

There was lots of razzing from the others when they picked blossoms from Carolyn's newly set-in plants and placed them on each table.

As Ben and David fooled around, Naomi and Barbara prepared a salad and Jim Thompson sliced bread and warmed it in the oven. It seemed that Carolyn had prepared potatoes ahead for the barbecue.

David wondered about two things. Were Barbara and

Ben going together? He was surprised when he saw Barb there and it soon became evident that Ben was sending out definite signals that she was his guest. One wife-to-be down, David thought wryly. He was also sort of curious about what Carolyn and Peter were doing.

Just as everyone was called for supper, Carolyn and Peter walked through the kitchen. David couldn't help overhearing Carolyn say, "I'm sorry, Peter. You're getting way ahead of me in math."

He smiled when Peter patted her arm as if to console her. "It's okay, Aunt Carolyn. Discussing math with you is still great." David wondered if there was any way he could help.

Supper was a pleasant affair. They feasted on barbecued chicken, Carolyn's delicious potatoes and Naomi's salad. Talk crisscrossed the table effortlessly. David found himself between young Peter and Jim. As the meal neared its end, he said to Peter, "I couldn't help overhear you say to your aunt that you had a math problem. Would you like me to take a look at it?"

David was amused when he observed that Peter was carefully scrutinizing him as if to discover whether David showed any signs of understanding math. David recognized that examination. He'd done it often when he was a kid, trying to estimate whether the kind adult offering assistance was capable or whether they would end up being upset by the fact that he was more knowledgeable than they.

Finally, the youngster nodded and said solemnly, "If you have time later, that would be great. Thank you, sir."

Charmed by his reply, David said, "After things are cleaned away, maybe we could find a quiet place. And by the way, my name is David."

As everyone rose to leave the table, Jim touched David's arm. "There are lots of people to clean up. Come and keep me company." He led David over to a pair of chairs on the deck where they could enjoy the sunshine streaking through the trees and watch Lynn and Peter playing another game of croquet.

As they settled, Jim explained, "The kids try not to be too obvious about it, but they work at saving me effort. Unfortunately, I tire quite quickly. However, I just learned last week from the heart specialist that there is a new and safer procedure that might allow them to tackle my heart problem. I'm going down to Toronto this week for tests. If everything is okay, they'll set a date."

They sat quietly for a few moments, watching the two children. Jim said, "Young Peter, there, is quite gifted. We're all anxious that he has the opportunity to develop his talents."

"Would mathematics be his subject?"

Jim looked surprised. "How did you figure that out?"

"I overheard him talking to Carolyn. I gathered they had been unsuccessful at solving a math problem. Maybe I can help."

When Jim looked as if he was about to warn him of the problem's difficulty, David assured him, "I have a doctorate in math. However, who knows. I may be a rotten teacher. But I told him I'd give it a try after everything is cleaned up."

"I didn't know that about you. Carolyn said you had a company and sold it. She indicated it had something to do with the electronic industry."

Then, Jim changed the conversation. "How do you feel the house is coming along? We are trying to finish it as quickly as possible. However, we were held up because the crew we usually use was booked until this week. They'll begin tomorrow to take over the work of Hugo and the boys."

David was sorry to hear that. He'd enjoyed working with the threesome. "Will you be letting them go?"

"No, Carolyn says they have been doing a great job. There are always jobs for two young pairs of hands. Part of the plan in hiring them was to let them experience the different trades. When they finish helping the Nortons complete the walls, they can help Ben with the plumbing. We plan to keep Hugo on and train him. I gather he is a reliable worker." There was a pause. "Anyway, it will free you up to do your own work."

Without thinking, David protested, "But I enjoyed working with them. I found it very interesting." And then something in Jim's expression made him pause.

Jim said, "I hear that you find it difficult to watch Carolyn climb a ladder. And," he paused for dramatic effect, "Ben says you have a foot fetish."

David could have wrung Ben's neck. When Jim just sat and waited, he tried to explain, "I know I've been acting like an idiot. For some reason, I just can't bear to watch her on a ladder."

Jim still said nothing but watched him with an interested expression. David finally confessed, "I have a fear of heights. Your deck is about as high as I go without suffering from vertigo. I walk close to inside walls when I have to climb open stairs like the ones in the house. Please don't tell anyone."

David watched Carolyn's father as he smiled, his blue eyes dancing. He seemed to be enjoying some secret thought. But he surprised David when he spoke. "Let me tell you about Carolyn. Better still, let me show you."

Still feeling foolish, David followed Jim across the

deck and through the kitchen past everyone hard at work. Jim led him down a hallway to his study.

Jim motioned him to a chair by an empty fireplace and then walked across to a row of photos on a bookcase. He picked up two and returned to sit down beside him.

He handed the first one to David. It showed Carolyn at eight or nine years of age. She wore a white T-shirt and bright red shorts and, to David's consternation, appeared to be walking along the ridge of a roof. Working with his back to her was a younger version of Jim, applying shingles. Even the picture had the ability to made David's stomach churn.

Before he could remark, Jim said, "Carolyn was like a little goat. Wherever I went when restoring this house, she was right beside me. My wife and I finally decided that it was safer to know where she was than to have her sneaking up to the roof or any other high surface by some devious route."

Handing David another picture, he said, "Take a look at this picture." This time it was one of Carolyn strutting along a fence after Ben who, as usual, was laughing. "The pair of them were terrors," Jim said fondly. "There was no keeping Carolyn away from what we were doing. But on the other hand, her desire to follow me around is how Carolyn picked up much of what she knows about construction and carpentry. She was an accomplished cabinetmaker before she finished high school."

David got the point of all the pictures. Jim was quietly telling him to quit bothering Carolyn when she was on a ladder. That she knew what she was doing.

Realizing that there was no defense for his behavior, he was about to change the subject when Peter knocked at the study door. When Jim told him to come in, Peter said, "David asked me to find him after everyone cleaned up. He's going to help me with my math."

"Well," said Jim, standing up. "You might as well work at my desk. There's plenty of room. Just drag a chair around, Peter." Then placing the pictures of Carolyn along the back of the desk, so that they would face Peter and David as they worked, he left.

David scowled at the pictures. He didn't need reminding that he was making a complete fool of himself over this ladder business. He received Jim's message loud and clear.

Carolyn drifted away from the kitchen when they had finished cleaning up. It was cooling off a little so she changed into slacks that matched her blue T-shirt and picked up a cardigan. Heading downstairs, she heard voices from her father's study. She was just about to walk in when she realized the voices she heard belonged to David and Peter.

Peter was speaking, obviously answering a question of David's. "A cryptogram is . . . hmmm . . . a secret message, like a code."

"Good for you, Peter. Can you think of any codes you know?"

Peter thought for a moment, then brightened. "Pig Latin. My buddy and I use it when we don't want my sister to know what we're talking about." He grinned. "It really makes her mad."

"Can you think of any other codes you know about?"

"Morse code."

"Good. Another question. Can you think of times when it is important to be able to use a code so that others don't know what you're communicating?"

Again Peter thought for a few moments, then answered. "Well, they'd use it in wartime. Also, I've read about industries using codes to keep their technologies secure."

Trust Peter to know about that, thought Carolyn.

David pulled the text Peter had been using toward him. "This chapter shows you an interesting way to create a code that is hard to decipher. It uses elliptic curves."

Carolyn remained at the door, unnoticed by the two of them. David's profile was slightly away from her while young Peter's face was clearly illuminated. He was completely engrossed in their conversation.

David leaned forward to write something down and the light struck his head. Feeling slightly guilty, she really studied him. He'd had his hair cut. Not short. But trimmed enough so that the curls looked carved on his head, like a Roman sculpture or a piece by Michelangelo. That thought took her imagination where she hadn't dared to go. He was wearing a soft summer sport shirt. As he moved toward Peter, the muscles rippled in his shoulders and arms and she could well imagine the symmetry of bone and flesh beneath his clothing. The image took her breath away.

At that moment, David turned toward her. His eyes, alive and glowing, held her. For seconds, she felt transfixed, caught in their brilliance. A current, thrumming with energy, ran between them and the hair on her arms and neck stirred.

In a panic, she turned and hurried out to the sunroom where the others had gathered. Settling in a corner, she tried to calm the beating of her heart and come to terms with the notion that somehow, everything about her, the room, her family, the very air she breathed, had altered, suffered some kind of change, so that nothing would ever be the same again.

She sat there, listening to Mike and Naomi, Ben and Barbara and her dad talk and watching Andy through the window set up fireworks to celebrate the holiday. And all the time, her thoughts scurried about, like a hamster on a wheel, never asking a question or getting an answer, simply refusing to understand what she felt. It was only when Peter came in that she was able to focus her attention away from her confusion.

"Auntie Caro. David showed me how to write a code, a really difficult code, using elliptical curves. He says that we should do lots together before I'll really understand them." He paused and reflected, then said modestly, "I think I do understand them actually."

She glanced around but David wasn't there. With a great sense of relief, she listened while Peter tried to explain how he made the code. When she felt the hair stand up on her neck, she knew that David had entered the room.

David stood at the door, watching, and listening with interest to all that Peter had to say. He is bright, he thought. Way ahead of me when I was his age. Then David's interest was snagged by a movement. Carolyn's leg was crossed and as she listened to Peter, she dangled her sandal off her toe. He'd never seen her barefoot before.

He watched with fascination as she moved the blue sandal about, stretching the highness of her arch and exposing the delicacy of her ankle. Images crowded his mind. Images of him holding that foot, stroking the fine bones. . . . He clamped down hard on his imagination. What was happening to him? He must be crazy. Praying for a distraction, he headed out to help Andy with the fireworks, far away from the source of any more way-ward thoughts.

It began to drizzle the next day when Carolyn drove up to the house to see how the Nortons were settling in. The team of four men worked efficiently. They wouldn't have any ceilings fall on them, she thought ruefully. They were far too experienced. She wandered about the second floor, checking the maze of small rooms in the one wing. Norton Senior was going over the area, checking the work that had been done. She was relieved when he said that they had done a good job.

Just then, she heard a vehicle drive up. Glancing out the window, she was surprised to see Ben and young Ted step out of the van. A moment later, David appeared and went off with Ted. Mystified, for Ben had told her he was doing another job while he waited for the interior of the house to be cleared, she headed for the stairs when she heard Ben clumping up them.

She was even more curious when Ben took her arm and pulled her into a small room she had designated as a bathroom. "Caro, I need your help."

That really surprised her. He needed her help? Surely not with plumbing. Maybe he'd run into a problem with Barbara. "Girl trouble?" she asked.

Ben's eyes lit up and he had trouble hiding a smug little grin. "Nothing to do with girls. Everything is just fine. No, I have a plumbing problem."

Carolyn couldn't hide her amazement. "Plumbing?"

"Well, not exactly plumbing." Ben rubbed the back of his neck and looked sheepish. "It's this way. David cornered me yesterday and asked if I would choose the fix-tures, tiles, and whatever else were needed for each of the bathrooms. He sort of suggested that he didn't want you to know he'd asked me. Admitted that he wasn't very good at making those kinds of decisions. Sort of strange when you consider that he's outside in the drizzle measuring the grounds around the house with Ted, and working away on a diagram that looks like a landscape drawing to me."

The devious devil, Carolyn thought. He said he'd make the bathroom decisions himself.

"Listen, Sis, I said I'd do it. But I really meant that I would get you to work out the design of each bathroom and the specifications. We need to get the various items ordered and out here. The Nortons are going to have this place finished in no time and I'll want to know where to set in the pipes. Andy's going to need to know about the wiring, especially if there's to be a Jacuzzi."

When Carolyn hesitated, Ben continued. "C'mon, Carolyn. David is a really important client. We need to do this job right. You know you've already placed all the washrooms in your model."

"You mean you were snooping around my workroom?"

"Since when has looking around your workroom ever been snooping?"

Carolyn shrugged. He was right, of course. It was just that everything about David Reid irritated her today. She'd been much too attracted to him the evening before and had lost a great deal of sleep trying not to let him worm his way into her dreams.

What Ben didn't know was that there was another design problem occupying her mind. The kitchen David had liked was not working out. Okay, it was alright but she had a better idea that would make a truly innovative kitchen. She'd just started working on a model. She'd have to give up on that idea until she designed the bathrooms. She supposed it didn't matter since this kitchen could never be made unless the cabin was returned to its original location and it looked like David was completely sold on the idea of the cabin staying where it was.

Ben interrupted her thoughts. "Carolyn, let your imagination go. Make them the bathrooms of your dreams. He keeps stressing money is no object. Go for it. Give him the best."

Carolyn couldn't help smiling. She gave him a gentle punch to the arm. "You're almost as bad as he is. Okay, I'll do it. It means I'm going to have to work like the devil if I'm to be ready for you when the Nortons are finished clearing everything out."

"And you won't tell David?"

"I won't, but on one condition. No more telling tales out of shop. No more kidding about foot fetishes. Okay?"

"Deal. Oh, by the way, don't forget that we begin to work on the scenery on Wednesday. Seven sharp." Innocently, Ben added, "David's coming. We'll keep him away from the ladders. He can paint."

Before she could object, her irrepressible brother hurried out and clattered down the stairs. Going over to the window, she watched as David and Ted walked about with a tape measure between them. Every now and then, they'd stop and David would make a notation on a clipboard. Finally, they finished and Ted went off with Ben. David disappeared out of sight in the direction of the cabin and she was able to slip out of the house and into her van.

Wednesday night, David walked into the local high school ready to assist with the scenery. A sign directed him toward the gymnasium. He arrived in time to see Ben, Barbara, and several others spreading out a large piece of canvas. A short, fair-haired man in T-shirt and shorts walked toward him. "You must be David Reid. I'm Henry Olsen. Glad you could come. We're just going to straighten this canvas on the floor and I'll sketch out the detail. This will only take me a few moments. Then, I'll set you to work with paint and brush."

David felt he had to explain. "I'm not much of an artist."

His fears were dismissed. "Don't worry. This is donkey work."

David caught Ben grinning at that. Little did Ben know how incompetent David felt. He couldn't draw a straight line without a ruler. Couldn't imagine how you'd sketch a scene, let alone paint it. He was beginning to feel like he did when Carolyn made him try to choose the wood samples.

Before he could convince himself that he should make a hasty exit, he was distracted by the entrance of Carolyn and her pal, Dan, lugging eight-foot two-by-fours. She wore workboots as usual, he noticed. They put down the wood and disappeared again.

David turned his attention to what Henry was doing. To his horror, he saw Henry draw a large tree in the foreground and behind, more trees with a path winding its way through them and disappearing behind a hill. David panicked. He was supposed to paint a tree?

As if sensing his new helper might bolt, Henry poured out green paint into a small can and handed it to David. "Ever do anything like this before?" he asked.

"Never."

"Well, don't worry. I'm going to show you exactly how to do this. First you're going to cover all this leaf area with this dark green. Later I'll show you how to do the leaves."

Leaves! He had to be kidding. However, David watched as Henry began to outline the leafy part of the tree he had drawn. "See. It's no more difficult than filling in the spaces in a coloring book. Just fill in the outline I've made."

David couldn't remember ever playing with a coloring book. However, he gingerly took the brush and squatting down, began to fill in the space. The paint went on quite easily and soon he began to feel a little rush of confidence and sense of satisfaction.

The others were given their assignments. They chattered and joked as they worked and David found himself actually enjoying himself.

The painters were working on the gym floor while Carolyn, Dan, and some others were working on the stage. She was directing the others. He could see that they seemed to be making three frames which looked like they might become walls. Down the hall, David could hear the voices of those in rehearsal. He reminded himself that Cindy had said they all met for coffee after their work session. Maybe he'd get a chance to chat with her.

At that thought, a burst of laughter from the stage caught his attention. There were two other fellows and a girl helping Carolyn and Dan. From what David could see, they were all laughing at the efforts of the team that had made one of the frames. Dan was shaking a corner where it was obviously poorly joined. Carolyn checked the joint and then said something. There were moans and groans as the pair working on the frame started to correct it and even more laughter.

As David watched, Carolyn stood up. Dan walked over to discuss the corrected framing. They both seemed very chummy.

David felt a spiral of annoyance at this thought. Ignoring this response, he returned to his green paint. With an effort, he concentrated on applying the paint but his joy in his accomplishment had faded.

The paint dried quickly. Soon David found himself doing the impossible, painting leaves. Now, this was really fun. Henry had given him a pie plate containing green of a lighter hue. All David had to do, Henry explained, was take the leaf-shaped sponge and pat on wedges of green that mimicked the shape of leaves. The others would come along and add lighter and darker shades where they were needed.

Soon David was experimenting. He'd place the wedges in groups, and other times arranged the leaves from one point. When Henry praised him on his inventiveness, David felt wonderful. How come he'd never learned the joys of daubing and playing with paint before? He answered his own question. His absolute fascination with mathematics had ruled out any fiddling around with other mediums. Well, it was never too late to learn.

When the paints were put away and order restored to the gym, the painters and builders joined the actors at the local coffee shop. Three tables were dragged together to accommodate them all.

As Carolyn sipped her coffee and nibbled on a doughnut, she watched and listened to the group. Barbara was describing her new car and praising a smugly pleased Ben. He caught Carolyn watching him and winked.

David had managed to sit beside Cindy while Dan sat on her other side. Fascinated, Carolyn saw that both Dan and David were busy chatting up Cindy. And Cindy, a very confident young woman, her curls bouncing and eyes sparkling as she answered the men's questions, was having a wonderful time.

A feeling of regret washed over Carolyn. She remembered when she had been just like Cindy, confident in herself and capable of enjoying the attention of eligible men. But since the episode with James, she had carefully avoided such light-hearted fun. Was that why it suited her to spend time with Dan? Was this the reason that Dan was so ready to spend what time he had from his practice with her? Had some experience in his past also made him extra cautious?

She took a bite of her doughnut and was about to lift her cup when she was suddenly aware that she was being watched. Glancing across the table, she saw that David was studying her as if trying to solve some puzzle. His very direct gaze made her uncomfortable and she remembered her reaction when she watched him with Peter. Again, she had that sense that the air had suddenly become charged. Uneasily, she smiled at him and broke eye contact. Finishing her coffee, she stood up and said good night to those present. To her surprise, David stood too and announced, "I'll walk you home, if that's alright with you. I want to find out how things are progressing in the house."

Glancing at Dan in case he wanted to leave, she found that he was lost in conversation with Cindy. Well, she thought, what do you know? Maybe Dan is ready to take flight. She fought down a sense of sadness. She enjoyed Dan's company and had grown to lean on him. But it was only right that she give him space if he wanted it. She must ask him. Meanwhile, she had to deal with David.

David preceded her to the coffee shop door and held it open for her. To exit, she had to slip by him. Uneasily, she moved past him, very aware of his scent, his height, and that he had paint on the hand that held the door.

She waited for him to exit, doing her best to tune out the effect he had on her. She concentrated on thinking about the spot of green paint instead. She'd been amused when she'd seen him painting, so like Peter when he was deeply involved with a problem.

She realized suddenly that David was walking along beside her, a puzzled look on his face. When she glanced at him, he asked, "Have I offended you?"

Startled, she told him exactly what she had been thinking. "I noticed you had paint on your hand. When you were painting you reminded me of Peter when he is working on a problem, completely focused."

David startled her by grinning sheepishly. "I've never painted before." Then almost as if surprised, "I really enjoyed it."

"Never?"

"Well, maybe I did in school as a kid, but if I did, I've totally forgotten about it." Then after a moment's silence, he admitted, "When I saw I was expected to paint, I nearly had a fit. But it was fun."

They strolled along the tree-lined street in silence for a few moments. Carolyn's senses seemed to be on full alert. She was conscious of the faint rustle of leaves above them and could smell the fragrance of lilacs from nearby gardens. She was totally aware of the man beside her, walking along, his hands in his pockets, waiting, it seemed, for her to speak.

"What was it you wanted to discuss with me, David?"

For the life of him, David could think of nothing to say. He was still trying to figure out what moment's madness had him walking out the door with her, carefully cutting out Dan who hadn't seemed to care. Desperately, he asked, "How are things coming along?"

He could tell from Carolyn's expression that she was surprised by his question. She knew he knew how they were coming along. He tried frantically to make it more pertinent. "I was wondering when they'd start to insulate?"

Carolyn wasn't quite sure what the question was leading to but she did her best to answer. "There's still a lot of work to do before we insulate. The Nortons have cleared specific areas so that Andy can work on the wiring and Ben can continue with the plumbing." Then some devil made her say, "I gather you liked Ben's plans for the bathroom joining the master bedroom. He thought you and your wife would enjoy the Jacuzzi."

Carolyn could have bitten her tongue for immediately an image formed of David in the Jacuzzi. What on earth was wrong with her? Glancing at David, she was amused to see that he was looking just a little uncomfortable. Recalling his deviousness, no doubt, she thought smugly.

David wondered. Had Ben given away his secret? Did she know he'd asked Ben to decide what was needed in the bathrooms? Whatever. He couldn't resist saying, "I've always thought a Jacuzzi provided a sense of romance to help keep a marriage alive." He grinned as he saw in the glow of the streetlight that she was blushing. So, she had an imagination too.

Grasping at straws, he tried to return to renovating. "Do you think I could help now and then? I promise I won't interfere. If you're going up a ladder, just tell me and I'll stay away. Your father informs me you're as agile as a mountain goat."

With that kind comparison, they reached her verandah steps. He found himself staring at her, suddenly conscious that he wanted to reach over and brush a wisp of hair from her face, even more conscious that he would like to taste the sweetness of her lips. He was unable to speak, not quite sure how to leave, so entranced was he with this idea.

It was Carolyn who broke the silence. "Thanks for walking me home, David. I'll think about your helping. To be honest, I don't think it's safe. I'll always be afraid you're going to come steaming in through a door, ready to haul me off the ladder. I find it distracting."

"And if I promise to leave you alone?"

"Can you do that?"

"I'll try."

Carolyn almost asked him why it was only her that he couldn't tolerate up the ladder but decided not to. Turning, she walked up the verandah steps. "I'll see you tomorrow. Good night, David."

He turned and headed back to the school where he'd parked his truck. He was still unable to explain why he'd felt he had to walk her home. Most of the time, she irritated him. Why, then, was she starting to live in his imagination?

## *Chapter Six*

Carolyn wandered over to the back door that opened out onto a tiny porch situated where the two wings joined the house. From here, she could see David. Early this morning a dump truck had arrived with a load of fine gravel. He'd wheeled load after load of the small stone down a path he had cleared to the lake. With each load, he meticulously shaped and smoothed a narrow lane; good for walking, wheeling a bicycle, or wheelbarrow.

You couldn't fault him for the effort he put into everything he did. There was nothing slipshod about his work any more than there was anything careless about his tennis playing. Why was it, she wondered with a smile, he couldn't make decisions about the house's interior?

She watched him as he wheeled down the last load he'd need before he reached the small sandy beach below. The light glistened on his back. Even from this distance, she could see the play of muscles as he steered the awkward load.

Closing her eyes for a minute to stop the rather inconvenient images that seemed to lurk in her mind, ever ready to distract her, she moved away from the window and returned to work.

Not long after that, she heard the rattle of another vehicle coming by the house. Curious, because she didn't expect any delivery, she was surprised to see a truck from a local company that made docking systems. As she watched, David greeted two men who hopped from the truck, then walked around to the back of the truck to help them unload stands for a portable dock. Soon the stands were loaded on a dolly and were being guided down David's new path.

When Carolyn and her crew stopped for lunch, she wandered out on the back verandah expecting to see the men working. To her surprise, the truck had left. Down under the trees, she could see a dock extending out from the shore, its metal frame glinting in the sunlight, a surface of cedar boards covering it.

Impressed with the speed with which the dock had been constructed, Carolyn decided to take her lunch and wander down to check it out. The path took her through a small meadow full of wildflowers—tall blue weed, white marguerites, orange devil's paintbrush, and buttercups, to the tree-lined edge of the lake. Here willows, silver maples, and birch clung to the shore. David's small beach was situated by a large willow. At the other end an irregular granite boulder, large enough to climb on, sat at the water's edge. Great for children, Carolyn thought.

Seeing no one around, Carolyn gave in to the temptation to cool off. Today, she was working in denim shorts and a cotton shirt, socks and workboots. It only took her a moment to shed her boots and socks and test the water with her toe.

David heard a sound and peeked around the curve of granite behind which he was sunning himself. Ah, he thought, my lady carpenter. As he watched, she stepped into the water, giving a little shiver as the coolness of the water lapped around her calves. She stood for a moment, letting her body acclimate and then moved out carefully. How utterly feminine she looked, he thought, as she stepped gingerly, her arms slightly bent, hands out for balance.

From the angle he watched, her reflection rocked gently before her as the noonday sun shone down through the trees, adding a sense of mystery; two women, one woman he knew, clear-headed, capable, and decisive; the other softer, romantic, beautiful, from some other place. Shaking his head to clear it of such whimsy, he decided he'd better speak up.

Standing up, he called, "Do you like my beach?"

At the sound of his voice, she nearly lost her balance. "Heavens, you scared me," she gasped.

"Sorry, I didn't mean to startle you. I thought you'd like to know I was up here. Didn't want you to think I was spying. Did you bring your lunch?"

She nodded.

"Well, cool off, then climb up here if you like. There's a natural seat in the rock. I'm just about to start my lunch. I'd enjoy the company."

Not sure whether she really wanted to spend time beside David eating her lunch, she procrastinated as long as she dared before clambering up the rock. To her relief, she found that he had changed to a swim suit and had on a white T-shirt. The brightness of the shirt only served to accentuate the golden tan that covered his muscled arms and legs.

As she settled down on the rock which curved in a right angle to him, he asked, "How do you like my beach?"

"It's great. Just the right size. Any bigger and the odd passerby might choose to use it. I'm impressed with the dock too. I couldn't believe you could get it assembled so quickly."

He pulled a sandwich out of a paper bag and took a bite. Reaching for a bottle of juice to wash it down, he said, "My new boat is being delivered this afternoon so I needed to be sure that everything was in place on time."

Carolyn had visions of a large speedboat with all the bells and whistles. However, she kept her thoughts to herself.

He added, "I'd like to learn how to fish."

"You've never been fishing?"

"Never had time." Then as an afterthought he asked, "Do you know how to fish?"

"With three brothers? You jest. I can put a worm on a hook with the best of them."

They ate silently for a while. It was pleasant on the rock. The tree dappled out enough shade to protect her head while letting her legs enjoy the full power of the sun. Eyeing her watch, she made a note of the time. She hadn't had much time to sunbathe this spring. It wouldn't do to burn. Next time, she'd bring her sunblock.

David finished his sandwich and leaned back. Picking up a soft cotton cap, he pulled it down over his forehead and surreptitiously watched Carolyn. She ate her sandwich delicately, savoring each mouthful and washing it down with bottled water. She finished her lunch with an apple.

As she munched on it, he was fascinated by the picture she made as she leaned over slightly, peering into a tiny pool of water on the rock. Light from the softly lapping waves sent glimmers of gold across her face and white shirt and along her long, elegant legs. She seemed unconscious of her loveliness, of the way a few tendrils of hair touched her cheek or of the slender line of her neck.

She leaned over to touch a finger into the tiny pool and as she did, her braid slid slowly down her arm. Unable to stop himself, David reached over and caught it. The slight pull caught her attention and she turned slightly to find him holding the end of her braid.

Surprised, she glanced up at him and wished she hadn't. It was as if a current raced between them along her plait of hair. Startled, she made to pull her head back to release her hair.

David felt the same surge of attraction and, in spite of a strong need to distance himself, was unable to give up his prize. He was determined to feel the lustrous ringlet that formed the end of the braid. He gave a gentle tug.

Her eyes flashed at this.

He teased, "I bet the boys were always putting your braid into an inkwell."

Carefully removing the braid from his hand, she reminded him, "There were no inkwells when I was in school." And then with a saucy grin, she asked, "Were there when you were a child?"

He shrugged and leaned toward the pool. "What were you looking for?"

"Dragonfly nymphs."

"Were there any?"

"No."

Feeling the need to break the tension she still felt between them, she said, "David. I really want to thank you again for helping Peter. He's progressed well beyond the mathematics I've studied. You can't believe how busy he is trying to make codes. Mike says he's been driving him nuts trying to get permission to come over to your place. Mike doesn't want him to become a nuisance. Besides, he hopes that he can get him interested in doing something else beside math this summer."

David could understand Peter's enthusiasm and his parents' concern. What had saved him from being completely immersed in mathematics as a kid was the expectation that he would help out in his parents' nursery in the summer.

"I've an idea that might answer all your problems. Any day now my family will be coming up with truckloads of stuff to complete the landscaping. I still have work to do to be ready for them. And when they come, I'll need assistance. Probably need it all summer. What would you think of Peter working up here for me and in exchange, I'll spend some time each day he comes answering his questions? I'll also pay him minimum wage for the time he works."

Embarrassed now, because her effort to change the subject had backfired, and it seemed as if she had been hinting to let Peter come up, she stood and said, "David, I wasn't suggesting that I wanted you to spend time with him. I was just telling you how he was doing."

David stood, too, sorry to end what had been a very pleasant interval. "Take it easy. I've had this idea for some time. Every time I see you I intend to ask you about it and then something comes up and I forget." When she looked doubtful, he said, "Honestly. I was actually going to phone Mike tonight. I really do need help. And I also need practice teaching. I'm going to be teaching part-time at Durham next fall. I've never done this before. Working with Peter will be good experience. Now, quit fussing and come down to the beach. I have another job for you."

David waited at the bottom of the rock and held out his hand. Warily, she took it and made her way down the rock, very aware of her reaction to his touch.

He walked toward the new dock. "I know you're very busy but do you think someone in your crew could take a few moments and make a small changing cabin? That way, when any of you are too hot and need a break, you could come down here, change, and take a dip."

"You wouldn't mind?"

"Why should I?"

Carolyn didn't have an answer for that.

"I've ordered some cedar picnic tables from the guy up the road. I thought I'd have one down here, one by the house and one by the cabin. I'm also expecting a canoe this afternoon when they deliver my boat. In time, I'll need a shed where I can store the motor and paddles. But I don't think there is a rush for that."

Just then, they heard someone calling down the hill. Looking up, Carolyn saw another delivery truck. "That must be your canoe. I don't see a boat trailer or boat."

She was surprised when he said, "The boat will be in the truck."

Sure enough, when they reached the top, Carolyn discovered a small aluminum boat and canoe propped in the back of the truck. So much for speedboats, she thought. What an unusual man. He always did the unexpected. What other man in these parts would settle for a small aluminum boat when he could easily afford the fastest speedboat available?

*   *   *

The next few days were very busy for Carolyn. The Nortons were still tearing out plaster and lath and had also undertaken the task of checking out the floors, getting the windows ready for removal and preparing for insulation. She was still undecided whether she should let David assist them; however, he hadn't raised the issue so maybe he had thought better of it.

She spent a lot of time in her workshop manufacturing pieces of trim that needed replacing. Whenever she came over to check the work in the house, she was amused to see Peter and David hard at work in the yard. Sometimes she'd step out onto the porch and listen for a few moments. Peter was always expounding on some problem he had although, to give the boy credit, he listened carefully when David gave instructions. Just as David promised, every afternoon they would disappear in his cabin where they "talked mathematics" as Peter gravely explained.

On Tuesday, when Carolyn usually tried to play tennis, she decided, instead, to return to David's house after supper to work on the staircase. It had been so scratched and worn over time that the surface needed refinishing. She also had something she wanted to show David if he was at the cabin when she finished.

Instead, David found her on that clear June evening. She didn't hear him until he actually walked into the hall.

"Thought you'd be playing tennis tonight."

"I wanted to begin sanding the staircase."

David frowned at that. "You don't need to have something as time-consuming as that done before I move in. It could be done anytime."

Carolyn flashed a smile at him. "Actually, I like sanding. It's very soothing and gives me time to think."

David walked over and removed the sanding block

from her hand. "Well, I've got a better occupation for thinking. Put your stuff away and come fishing. You said you were an old pro. And I understand this is a good time of day to catch fish."

Taking a look outside, she saw that he was right. It was tempting. The lake below was calm and the warm light of evening lit its surface.

Why not? she thought. They'd both be gainfully employed so that the nerve-racking electricity that sometimes seemed to crackle between them should not be a problem.

"Okay. But first, let me show you something. It's in the van."

David followed her out of the house quite pleased with himself. He'd always wanted to fish from a little boat just like the one he'd bought. And he was sure Carolyn would be a good teacher. Also, he had to admit, he really enjoyed Carolyn's company when she wasn't irritating him.

Curious to see what she had in the van, he caught up with her as she took a small box out of the back. Carefully, she lifted out a small model of a shed and carried it over to the new picnic table where she set it down. The miniature shed was about eight inches high and had a rectangular base. Its peaked roof was covered with metal just as he expected the house would be. Its tiny gable was trimmed with the same gingerbread pattern that trimmed one of the house's gables.

David couldn't help but reach out and touch the roof. The model was exquisite. Every detail was perfect. Before he could remark on the model, Carolyn said, "I had this idea for your shed and changing room."

Reaching over, she opened two doors that were on one side of the shed. David saw that the interior was divided into two cubicles, just right for changing. Even tiny hooks were set in the wall. Pointing at the spaces, Carolyn explained, "On this side of the shed, you have two changing rooms."

She turned the shed around and opened two more doors. He saw this half of the shed was for the storage of paddles and supplies. There was even a little rack he guessed was for his motor.

Carolyn explained, "I thought the beach really wasn't large enough for two sheds. This one can fulfill both functions. What do you think?"

To her surprise, David didn't answer. Instead, he picked up the model and studied it carefully. He fingered the details gently. Then turning to her, he said, "This is wonderful. When did you ever find time to make it?"

"It's my hobby. I've made models for years. I test all my ideas out in models first. Do you really like it?"

David sensed her uncertainty about the model as well as her design. "May I keep this?"

Carolyn was confused. "Keep it? Why?"

"Because it's exquisite. I had no idea you have such talents." And then, aiming a smile that startled her, he added, "The shed's perfect. C'mon. Let's go fishing. I've got rods, worms, and everything else I could think of."

Following him to his truck, she was amused to see that he came fully equipped; no less than four fishing poles, a fish bucket, a net, and a container of worms. Selecting two rods, David explained, "I bought extra fishing poles. When my family visits, I expect that some of the kids will want to fish."

Bemused, she followed him as he hurried down the path to the beach, a net and bucket in her hands. He was absolutely dancing with anticipation. She prayed to the god of fishermen that he might catch a fish.

Carolyn expected that they would use the motor delivered at the same time as the boat. Instead, he pulled two oars out from where he had hidden them in the bushes. "I think it's best if I have my first fishing lesson when the boat is still, don't you?"

Carolyn couldn't help asking, "You do swim, don't you?"

Handing her a life jacket, he assured her, "In Toronto I swam a mile twice a week."

"I'm impressed," she admitted.

Together, they prepared to shove off. David took the oars. "Where to?"

Carolyn suggested they row over to an area where the odd lily pad floated on the water's surface. Moving to the bow, she settled down to watch David. Surprisingly, it only took him a few minutes to achieve a rhythm so she sat back to enjoy herself.

It was one of those June evenings when the sky was a vivid blue. The setting sun illuminated the opposite shore so that every rock, tree, cottage, and boathouse stood out in purest hues, their color illuminated in the lake's reflection. They moved along the shore, cutting through the sky's reflection, leaving a dark "V" of gentle waves working their way across the lake to the other side.

Once David had chosen a place and thrown over the anchor, he handed her a fishing rod and the container of worms.

Surprised because she was sure he would want to get his line ready first, she took the rod, loosening the hook and fished out a worm from the container. As she efficiently impaled the hapless worm on the hook, she glanced up. His face was a study. She could swear that he gritted his teeth as she fed the worm along the hook. He was squeamish!

Chuckling to herself, she handed him the other pole and after he loosened the hook, held out the open worm container.

She watched him swallow as he gingerly picked up a nice juicy worm that squirmed helplessly between his fingers. He brought the hook toward the worm and then hesitated. He actually shuddered. "Heavens, Carolyn, you have to be a kid of six or seven to be bloodthirsty enough to do this."

"Pretend you're Peter's age and do it. After all, you intend to eat the fish. What's the difference?"

Shutting his eyes, he stuck the hook in the worm. "Feed it along the hook," she instructed.

He gave her a baleful look and with another shudder, fed the worm on the hook.

She couldn't help but laugh. "I can't believe you've never done that before." When he threw the hook in the water, she said, "See, it wasn't that bad, was it?"

"You may laugh," he said, "But you have to take the fish off the hook. I hope it's a great big pike with shark teeth. Then we'll see who's laughing."

She showed him how to send the line out and slowly wind it in, and after awhile, they both settled into a steady rhythm. Neither talked. They were surrounded by sound. A bullfrog croaked close by, a duck quacked in the nearby reeds, and a great blue heron moved languidly along the shore, ignoring them completely as it stopped and waited to snatch its prey.

"It will probably catch my fish," David whispered.

Carolyn didn't really care if she caught a fish. It was the first time since they'd taken on David's renovation that she'd done anything on the spur of the moment. As dusk settled across the lake, she relaxed. She couldn't help wondering about the man across from her. He had been so against her when they'd first met.

Without meaning to, she whispered, "David. Why were you so upset when you found that I was in charge of your renovations?"

In the gloom, she saw that he was looking at her, weighing his answer. Finally, he said, "I had a bad experience with a woman foreman during my first summer job. She made my life miserable—and she wore workboots."

"Workboots?" Carolyn repeated, not quite understanding the significance.

"I'm afraid that when I see a woman wearing workboots, I overreact. I expect her to behave like Linda. It took me awhile to realize that you were nothing like her."

"Do my workboots bother you now?"

"Not in the way you'd think. Now, I can't believe it's possible that someone can look so s . . . er, attractive wearing them."

That shut her up. She knew the word he'd been going to use was sexy. Funny, she thought, she hadn't thought of herself as sexy for a long time. Not since James. Dan had certainly not seen her as sexy. Oh, he'd thought she was attractive, and always complimented her, but she knew that he simply had not had that reaction to her.

David hastily drew in his line after that confession and concentrated on whipping it through the air so that it would go farther. I must be losing my grip, he thought. I almost told Carolyn she was sexy. I don't want to think of her as sexy. I want to find a tiny woman, delicate, maybe fair-haired, someone vivacious, and of course, sexy.

The trouble was, he couldn't even imagine such a creature, not with Carolyn facing him in the dusk, her long jean-clad legs stretched out before him, the faint fragrance she always wore drifting across the space between them.

A sudden tug on his line distracted him. Sitting up, he whispered urgently, "I've got a bite. What do I do now?"

"Reel him in gently. Let him take a little run and reel him in some more."

Given the chance, the fish shot off, pulling the line through the reel. "Bring him in again," instructed Carolyn.

David and the fish worked for a few minutes. It was soon obvious that David would win. When he finally hauled the fish out of the water and into the net Carolyn held, he let out a yell of triumph.

Carolyn realized that in the darkness, he would find it difficult to take the fish off the line and took mercy upon him. She eased the fish off the hook and dropped it in the wire fish basket, then threw the basket back into the water. "Next time you have to take it off the line," she warned.

Taking a flashlight, David pulled up the basket and shone a light on the fish. "What kind is it? Is it long enough to keep? Can I eat it for breakfast?"

"Only if you have the stomach to clean it. And don't ask me to. My brothers always did that part. Oh, and by the way, it's a perch."

In the end, they caught three more fish between them. Two were thrown back and two were kept for breakfast. By the time Carolyn left for home, she knew that David was one tired but happy fisherman.

When Carolyn returned home, she noticed her workboots sitting neatly by the back door. So he didn't like girls in workboots, she thought. Unable to stop the grin of mischief that spread across her face, she picked up her boots and carried them out to her workshop.

Going over to her work bench, she selected several small bottles of paint. After getting a container of water and brushes, she placed her boots on the work table. Humming to herself, she began to paint pink flowers and green leaves all over the surface of the toes. She painted an ivied branch of leaves up the sides of the boot ending with delicate yellow blossoms. She studied the effect for a few moments, cleaned up her brushes, put away her bottles of paint, and headed back to the house with her boots.

As she climbed the stairs for bed, she enjoyed a pleasant sense of satisfaction without allowing herself to analyze why it was so necessary for David Reid to realize that she was not like his former boss.

## Chapter Seven

The next morning, feeling a little bit silly now, Carolyn drove up to the house wearing her decorated boots. Hopping out of the van, she looked for signs of David, hoping to catch his reaction when he saw her boots. Then she heard the sound of a motor starting and, glancing down the hill, saw the small boat leave from the dock, her intrepid fishing student at the helm. Oh well, she thought, it can wait. I wonder if he'll get the point.

She was hard at work framing the walls of the two rooms and bathroom off the kitchen when she heard a truck approach. Curious, she walked out on the verandah to find the men who were to replace the metal roof. Used to dealing with the unexpected arrival of tradesmen, she left what she was doing and went out to greet them.

Archie and Angus MacDougall were two Scots who had not lost their accents even though they left Scotland twenty-five years before. Archie was a tall well-built redhead with the bluest eyes she had ever seen. Angus was as dark as his brother was fair and viewed the world from the same bright eyes.

Archie dipped his head shyly and said, "I hope you don't mind, lassie. We just wanted to measure the roof."

Carolyn peeked around the side of the house and saw that David was still fishing. It would be safe to climb the ladder. Turning to the two men, she said, "Sure Archie. We'll need to place safety boards as we go. I see you've got your ladders."

"Aye. I've also cut the boards to nail down."

She watched as the two men assembled their ladders and secured them safely. With another guilty glance down toward the beach to assure herself the coast was clear, she headed up the ladder after the two men. As the boards were just over one inch square and six feet long, she carried two of them in one hand.

By the time she reached the top, Archie was already standing and Angus was squatting near the edge waiting for her to hand him the planks of wood. Quickly and efficiently the three of them worked their way up the roof, nailing down slats every fifteen inches. The men did most of the work while Carolyn ferried the wood up the ladder. Finally, the men fastened a line around the chimneys at either end of the gable and Carolyn walked up the slats to hand them the safety lines.

She'd worked with the men before on the Hepburns' house and felt completely confident with the routine. She handed one line to Angus and was about to fasten her own to the safety line before heading to the other end of the roof to hand Archie his line, when she made the mistake of looking down over the lake. To her horror, she saw David starting up the path.

In the second her attention wavered, her toe caught on a loose piece of metal roofing. With a cry of alarm, she tried to get her balance. At the last second, she threw herself in Archie's direction. With the agility of a mountain goat, he was beside her, one hand on the safety rope between the chimneys and the other clasping her arm.

Because of his grip, she fell forward, sliding down the roof until her toes caught the edge of one of the wooden slats. Between Archie and herself, they stopped her descent. In seconds Angus was across the roof and steadying both of them.

"M' God, lassie. Are you alright?" gasped Archie.

Carolyn lay there for just a moment, trying to catch her breath and calm her racing heart. All she could do was nod.

"Angus. Help her down to the ladder," Archie ordered. "We'll finish ourselves."


David started up the path, absolutely delighted with his catch of a sizable fish. He paused for a moment to admire his house standing proudly at the top of the hill. The sun glinted off parts of its rusted metal roof. Its angles and gables looked regal against the blue sky, its peach-colored bricks warm and welcoming.

Just as he was about to continue up the hill, he saw two men's heads and shoulders appear above the ridge pole. They seemed to be tying something around the chimneys. Even that action made his stomach shift uneasily. Then, he saw Carolyn appear with the men.

To his absolute horror, he saw her suddenly appear to teeter. Her arms flew out for balance and then, she disappeared.

Dropping his fish David ran, faster than he had ever run in his life. Carolyn, his beautiful Carolyn was falling. In his mind he could see her sliding backwards off the roof, drifting slowly, like a diver in a backflip, her beautiful hair floating about her and then, ending the maneuver with a sickening thud.

Charging around the corner of the house, he expected to see a crumbled clutter of arms and legs. Instead he saw Carolyn backing sedately down a very tall ladder. The sight of her alive and unhurt sent a surge of irrational anger through him and he headed for her like a heat-seeking missile, ready to explode on contact.

Carolyn was still trembling as she stepped carefully down the ladder. Her teeth were chattering with her near miss; her mind filled with images of what might have happened. She saw herself sliding head first down the roof's grade, her fingers frantically scrabbling for a grip on the safety boards. She could see the slide over the eave trough, her fingers unable to grip it and then the long, merciless plunge to the hard earth below.

More thoughts crowded her mind. Her fall would surely have caused her father's death. Guilt swept over her. She should have been more careful. If only she hadn't glimpsed down and seen that dumb David Reid. Illogically, she fumed, it was all his fault.

Suddenly, he was literally in her face, hauling her off the ladder and yelling abuse. She heard the words, "Stupid, stupid woman" and went off like a rocket. Who did he think he was calling her names? It was all his fault.

They were both beside themselves, both distraught, both screaming insults and neither listening to the other.

Finally he yelled, "Shut up, just shut up" and before Carolyn knew what was happening, she found herself trussed up in his arms, unable to avoid his angry mouth.

It was a kiss of punishment, of intense male fury, and she exploded in response; equally as angry, equally eager to punish, to give as good as she was getting. There were

no stars, no pleasure, just a self-righteous need to dom-
inate.

Gasping for breath, they looked at each other, as
shocked by their kiss as by her near fall, then David
cupped her face with trembling hands and whispered,
"Carolyn, I thought I was going to find you a heap of
broken bones on the ground. I thought I'd lost you." And
he was kissing her again, and this time, there was only
joy and release as they shared a kiss of such intensity
that both were shaken beyond endurance.

Suddenly, Carolyn realized that she was melded to one
highly amorous male, the very one that had caused her
predicament, and her anger returned. "Let me go," she
spit. "Don't ever touch me again. Get out of my sight."

And shaking off his grip, she stormed to her van.
Jumping into it, she started it, slammed it into gear,
spewed gravel as she shot down the lane, and disappeared down the concession road.

David was left, gripping the ladder, trying to make
sense of what had just happened. He looked up at the
sound of throats clearing and was horrified to discover a
man at the top of each ladder eyeing him with avid interest.

All his anger focused again, this time on Archie and
Angus. Backing up so he could really see them, he
yelled, "What did you think you were doing letting her
up on that roof? That metal's as slippery as glass."

"Ms. Thompson's as fleet o' foot as a mountain goat.
Something distracted her."

Guilt washed over David and his anger turned inward.
Without a word he headed back down the path, past his
fish still on the ground, to the beach. Pulling off his
runners, he charged into the lake and, mindless of safety,
began to thrash his way across the bay, each stroke let-

ting off some of the frustration building from his fright, their argument, their kiss, and his guilt.

Carolyn only made it a half mile down the road when she burst into tears and had to pull the van over. Folding her arms on the steering wheel, she wallowed in a fit of self-righteous indignation spiced with a good deal of guilt and remembered terror.

Back on the roof, Archie grinned at Angus. "Looks like wee Carolyn has met her man."

"Aye, I think you'd be right."

David sat in his small aluminum boat, hunched over his motionless oars, brooding, his fishing rod flat on the bottom of the boat. A mist hung over the water, muffling sounds. Even the frogs and ducks remained quiet. The silence suited him. He needed to think.

He halfheartedly gave the oars a tug and sent the small boat slipping over the smooth surface of the lake and then leaned on the oars again. His thoughts were getting no further than his boat, he thought.

For the first time in his life, his intellectual powers were letting him down. All his carefully laid plans for home and family were falling apart. There would be no petite blond in his life, the mother of his children. Not one of his ideas about a wife mattered because the decision had been taken right out of his hands. He loved Carolyn Thompson. She of the great workboots and the predilection for ladders had his heart completely.

He couldn't figure out exactly how this had happened. He'd had women in his life before. There'd been two serious relationships in his adult life; each ended amicably.

Not only that, he'd been pursued by lots of women. The minute his business became a success there was no end to the line of interested women; career women, society climbers, women after wealth.

But he'd always known what he wanted. He wanted a family life just like the one he had growing up. His parents were still in love and had created a home in which he and his brother and sister, different as they all were, had grown up loved and confident in themselves. He wanted a home like the one he'd been raised in.

He had been so busy pursuing some sort of schoolboy dream that he'd been blind to the fact that Carolyn had all the qualities he valued. Her big clumping boots had been a red herring. They had constantly reminded him of the dreaded Linda.

He rubbed his hand wearily across his forehead. Today, he'd probably blown his chances with her. Screaming at her, grabbing her, and kissing her angrily were hardly ways to endear himself. Recalling those kisses, he brightened. That second kiss had been really something. She'd been with him all the way.

A small wind rippled the water and the mist began to lift. The air freshened and with it, his spirits. What on earth was he doing out here rowing in circles? Surely someone who could solve problems in math and electronics should be able to solve matters of the heart.

He gave the oars another tug. Who was he kidding? He was going to have to face his own fears before he could contemplate pursuing Carolyn. He had already endangered her by making her nervous when he was around. He believed her when she said it was his fault she'd slipped on the roof.

David knew what he had to do before he could even begin to win her affections. He had to cure himself of this horrible phobia, but the very thought of doing so sent a chill down his spine. He acknowledged with a grimace that he would first have to purchase a ladder. It might as well be an extension ladder, he thought. I can work through this problem in stages; start with the verandah roof and aim for the main roof later.

*Chapter Eight*

Carolyn woke the next morning, still unsettled from her experiences of the day before. She wasn't sure what bothered her more—her carelessness on the roof or the incredible abandon with which she'd kissed David. One thing she knew for sure was that she had no intention of going out to that house today. She'd go to Smithboro or even Peterborough and find the tiles she wanted for one of the bathrooms.

When she wandered downstairs she found her father already sitting at the table drinking coffee. He greeted her with a smile and observed, "Slept in today, I see. Are you sure you're not working too hard? It seems to me you're at that house or in your workshop all the time."

Walking over and giving her dad a kiss, she assured him, "I'm fine. I plan to go to Peterborough to see if I can get some bathroom tiles. Want to come?"

"I don't think so. I think I'll stick around in case the

doctor calls about those tests I had in Toronto. I figure I should hear today or tomorrow."

Carolyn filled her cup with coffee and sat down opposite her father. She studied his face, looking for new signs of illness. "How are you feeling, Dad? Really?"

Her father reached out and took her hand. "I'm feeling reasonably well, love. Not any worse. But I'm hoping the chance for the new procedure comes through. I'd love to have my old energy back."

Not exactly reassured, Carolyn helped herself to cereal already on the table.

"I'm glad you're going to town," her father said. "It's going to be a scorcher today. You'll be cooler in the van and in the stores."

Used to each other's company, they ate their breakfast silently. Suddenly, her father started. "I forgot. A parcel from the florist came for you this morning." Getting up, he walked over to the refrigerator and lifted out a long white box decorated with a big red bow.

He watched as Carolyn wordlessly took the box and set it down beside her. She hesitated for a moment, suddenly very sure she knew who it was from.

Realizing that her father was waiting, she loosened the bow and lifted the lid. Inside was an assortment of summer perennials; delphinium, larkspur, cosmos, Shasta daisies, snapdragons, baby's breath.

She couldn't help herself. She reached over and touched the flowers' silky petals. They were all her favorite flowers. And all ahead of the season.

Her dad whistled softly. "They must have come up from the States. They certainly aren't in bloom around here yet."

A card was wedged into the mass of blossoms. Picking

it up, she opened it carefully. Just as she had expected, the flowers were from David. The note said:

*Forgive my loutish behavior. I'm sorry I distracted you. David.*

Carolyn carefully put the note back in the envelope and tucked it in her pocket. "It's from David," she explained to her father. "We had a little spat yesterday. He's apologizing."

Jim watched his daughter grab a section of the newspaper and busily eat her cereal. He noted the sudden flush that graced her cheeks and smiled.

For some time he'd thought that Carolyn and David were on a collision course, but was sure neither of them knew it. Ever since David had admitted that he couldn't stand to see Carolyn on a ladder, he'd suspected that he cared for his daughter more than he realized. On the other hand, he wasn't sure how Carolyn felt about David.

Jim liked David and hoped something would come of their attraction. He would feel much better if she was settled. He wouldn't admit it to her but he was feeling more fatigued all the time. He wasn't sure how much time he had, especially if he wasn't suited for the new surgical procedure.

Then he remembered the lovely little model she'd made. "How did David like the model of the shed?"

He wasn't prepared for the absolute glow in her eyes when she answered, "He said it was exquisite and asked if he could keep it."

Jim's opinion of David rose another notch. Carolyn was very prickly about the models she made. He'd never discovered why. Possibly they had been criticized when she'd been away at university although, he thought with a father's pride, it would be hard to see what some architectural professor could find wrong with them.

It was 3:00 by the time Carolyn returned from Peterborough. Picking up a plastic shopping bag, she headed up the stairs of the verandah when she noticed her father sleeping on the chaise lounge. As always when she saw him sleeping, she had a moment's panic. He was so still. Then she saw that his chest was rising and falling and that his sleep was natural. It amazed her that he could stand the heat. However, she knew that he felt cold, even on the hottest day.

Entering the hall, she had almost reached the stairs when the telephone rang. Racing to the nearest phone, she managed to pick it up before it woke her father. The last thing she expected to hear was David's voice. There was something strange about it when he said hello.

Still sensitive about the events of the previous day she answered abruptly, "What can I do for you, David?"

"There's a small emergency out here." Then the sound on the phone wavered.

"I can't hear you David. Did you say there was an emergency?"

Again the sound was distorted. She was only able to pick up the words "come right away" before the connection faded.

Glancing out at her father on the porch, she was relieved to see that he was still asleep. No use upsetting him, she thought, as she raced up the stairs and threw the bag with its contents on the bed where green fabric spilled out over the white bedspread.

She ignored her purchase and, because it was so hot, grabbed a light T-shirt and shorts and quickly changed. Putting on a pair of socks, she hurried downstairs, pulled on her workboots and tied them, grabbed her purse, and hurried out the back door so that her father wouldn't hear her leave.

As she headed up the street, she racked her brains, trying to think what kind of emergency could have occurred. Surely, the Nortons were there.

David closed the cell phone and lay back on the roof, his arm over his face. If the vertigo he suffered every time he sat up didn't finish him, the sun would. He'd tried to reach both of Carolyn's brothers. Phoning her had been his last resort. So much for brave deeds, he thought ruefully.

Carolyn raced up the lane and stopped beside the house. No one was in sight. Where were the Nortons? Their truck should have been there. Only David's truck stood in front of the house.

Hopping out of the van, she walked around the house toward the verandah as she called his name.

No answer. She was about to call again when she realized that an extension ladder was set up against the verandah. Why had the Nortons put a ladder up there? She hurried to the verandah and called again, louder this time.

"Up here."

Up where? she wondered. And then she remembered the ladder. Stepping back, she was astonished to see David lying flat on his back on the verandah roof, his feet almost touching the eaves, his arm over his face.

As she watched, he struggled to sit up and she saw him actually sway before he collapsed back on the hot metal.

Her first thought was that he must have fallen off the

main roof. Absolute panic had her rattling up the ladder and kneeling beside him on the hot metal.

He lifted his arm from his flushed face, showing lines of stress etched deeply. Perspiration trickled down it. His curls clung damply to his skull. She reached over and touched his forehead. He was burning up.

"Could you get me a drink of water?" he croaked. "Better still, a pail of water to throw over my head."

She understood immediately that he wasn't joking and scrambled down the ladder and over to the cabin. Luck was with her and she found a pail right away. Filling it, she grabbed a plastic glass and a cloth, and headed back to the verandah roof.

When she was beside him, she braced the pail against herself and tried to lift his shoulders to let him drink from the glass. He struggled up himself but she noticed he kept his eyes closed. With trembling hands, he took the glass and swallowed the contents. Lying back, he opened his eyes again.

"What were you doing on the roof?" she demanded.

He grimaced. "Trying to slay a dragon."

"A dragon?"

"Please, Carolyn. Have mercy on me. Pour some water over my head."

Carolyn gently trickled water over his head but saved enough for another glass. He took a huge breath and before her eyes, his color improved.

Very curious now, she demanded, "What do you mean, you were slaying dragons?"

He lay there for a moment without answering and she began to worry again if he was suffering from sunstroke. Then without warning, he turned his head toward her and whispered, "I'm afraid of heights."

Even more confused now and still fretting about the

heat, she asked, "Well, if you're afraid of heights, why on earth were you up this ladder?"

He reached up with his hand and brushed a strand of hair that curled around her face. That strange sense of connection happened again. It was as if they were surrounded by energy. Startled and uneasy by her reaction, she eased back on her heels and whispered, "Why?"

"I wanted to prove I could overcome my fear. I didn't want to be the cause of another accident. I nearly lost you yesterday."

Carolyn was ashamed of herself. All she could think of was that her bad temper had made him take an unnecessary risk. Impulsively, she grabbed his hand. "David, my own carelessness caused my accident. I know better than to try and do more than one thing at a time when I'm on a roof."

He tightened his grip and shook his head. "I want to be able to watch you walk on a roof. I want to enjoy seeing you climb a ladder. I hate this phobia I've developed." He tried to sit up but she pushed him back. Taking the cloth from the pail, she trickled water over his face and down his throat. "I saw you try to sit up before and you swayed. Are you dizzy?"

Looking away from her, he muttered, "Only when I try to get up. You're going to have to help me, Carolyn. I don't think I can get down on my own."

She poured the rest of the water into the glass and again he kept his eyes closed while he drank. He seemed cooler now and his breathing was slower.

"Do you think you can open your eyes now?"

"I'll try. Before I suffered vertigo. Give me your hand."

Carolyn felt a light tremor when she took his hand. Then he opened his eyes and looked at her. He looked away from her and she felt him lurch. Switching his gaze back to her he said, "I'm alright if I look at you rather than out over your head. I think I might be able to turn over and wriggle onto the ladder if you'll stay at the top of the ladder and let me watch you."

Carolyn waited helplessly as he rolled over on his stomach and then hunched up on all fours before the ladder. When she would have helped him, he muttered, "Leave me to my dragon."

The descent was the hardest thing David had ever had to do. Raising his body enough to get out and around the ladder was terrifying but he made it. And all the time, he watched Carolyn. He expected to see scorn on her face but instead he saw only concern. Inch by inch he eased down the steps until finally, he reached the ground. He stood at the bottom of the ladder for a moment, his eyes closed and muttered, "So much for slaying dragons."

Carolyn came down the ladder to stand beside him. He glanced at her face expecting to see criticism and instead saw approval. She astonished him by saying, "That's the bravest thing I've ever seen anyone do."

David felt her words of praise flow over him. He experienced a sudden easing, an untying of the knot of fear he had carried within him for so long. Looking up at the ladder, its distance didn't seem so far. Maybe he'd try to climb it another day.

Grabbing David's hand, Carolyn pulled him toward her van. "C'mon. I think I can drive down to the beach. You need to cool off."

Reaching the beach, they removed their boots. Carolyn walked beside him, watching to see that he was steady. David took the first few steps cautiously and became aware that Carolyn was still standing behind. Exhausted as he was, he still had no intention of swimming without Carolyn sharing the experience.

Glancing back, he held out his hand. "Come with me."

She hesitated for a moment and then placed her hand in his and together, they moved slowly forward until the water reached Carolyn's shoulders and his chest.

David thought that every horrible moment on the roof had been worthwhile when he turned and watched her. She was like some water sprite. Her ponytail had come undone and fanned out across the water. Holding her blue gaze, he slowly began to sink. With a smile, she decided to play the game. Together the let the water cover their necks, then their chins and finally, still holding hands, they ducked together.

Breaking the surface they floated on their backs, hardly moving. A halo of heat haze seemed to hover over them. The sound of a cicada nearby entranced them. In the distance an oriole whistled.

David felt like he could float forever. The moment was sublime. One he knew he'd never forget. Gripping her hand more tightly, he turned his head enough to see her face. She turned toward him and smiled. He fought down the desire to stand and haul her against him, to claim her lips, to fuse their wet bodies together and to declare his love. But he held back, not sure of her feelings.

Finally, without speaking, they ended their idyll and stood together. Concerned, she asked, "How do you feel now?"

His grey eyes lit with an expression she had never seen before. "Wonderful," he said. Together they moved toward the shore, the water sheeting off their bodies.

Still dripping, they sat side by side, pulling on their workboots. It was while Carolyn was lacing hers that she sensed he was watching. Glancing up, she saw the silliest grin on his face. When she raised her eyebrow in question, he teased, "Since when do workboots come decorated with flowers. Hateful Linda never wore them, that's for sure."

Standing with as much dignity as she could muster, she snapped, "Well, I'm nothing like Linda."

"Thank heaven for that," he said fervently. "I love your boots."

He walked behind her as they headed back to the van, enjoying the sway of her sopping shorts and the glint of afternoon sun on her long legs. It had been a great day after all.

As David changed for supper, before showing up at the gym to paint again, he thought about Carolyn. He wondered if she'd been hurt some time in the past. From the very first day, she had reacted negatively to him in spite of the unquestionable chemistry that existed between them. Even today on the roof when he'd touched her face, she had jerked back. Oh, she had tried to hide her reaction, but it had been there.

If that was the case, he wondered how she'd be when he saw her tonight. When they entered the lake hand in hand the magic had begun. The entire experience had been almost spiritual, a blending of souls. He'd felt at one with her; something his mathematical self had never experienced before. He was sure that the moment had been just as real for her. The question was, would they still share the same feelings when they met again? He knew he would, but would she?

Carolyn stood under the shower, shivering in spite of the warm water, letting it pour over her as if to wash away the effects of the afternoon. She needed to rid herself of the tempting sense of oneness she'd shared with David; needed to shake the impression he'd made when he struggled down that ladder. Most of all, she had to forget the overwhelming anguish she experienced when she'd thought he'd been hurt on the roof.

She could feel herself moving into dangerous territory. He had touched her heart, climbing that ladder when he was so obviously terrified of heights, and doing it for her. Did he care that much for her, and how did she feel about him? Was there more to it than just her uncomfortable awareness of him? She closed her eyes in despair. She had no confidence in herself and her judgment when it came to the motivations of men. She had been so wrong about James.

How did one identify love? She'd been so amused by David's naïve idea that he could just fall in love. But her own understanding of the emotion was no better. She wanted this man, needed to touch him, to cling to him, but had no idea if it was love. At least David had faith that he would fall in love whereas she wouldn't recognize love if it was right under her nose.

The way he affected her made her anxious. She didn't need this attraction right now. There were too many other things to worry about. Even though her father tried to hide it, he was getting weaker every day. She needed to have everything moving smoothly at David's house so her father wouldn't worry. Any influence that kept her from doing her best would only add to his stress. Let's face it, she thought, David Reid is in my thoughts far too much. It would be all to easy to make another mistake and have another accident.

Deciding that the best decision was to put some distance between them she hurriedly dressed for supper.

*       *       *

When David entered the gym, he was surprised to see some of the painters and builders in a huddle listening to an excited Ben. Curious, he was about to join the group when someone moved and he noticed Carolyn's face. In spite of her smile, she was as white as a sheet. Something had definitely happened to upset her. And Dan was standing beside her, his arm protectively around her.

Why Dan? he thought. Why couldn't it be him?

Determined to find out what was going on, David walked over. Barbara turned to him. "I guess you haven't heard the good news. Ben's dad has been accepted for the experimental surgery. He just found out this afternoon. He's to leave next Wednesday, a full five days before his surgery."

David turned to Carolyn. "I'm so glad Carolyn. How's your dad taking it?"

"He's absolutely thrilled."

But David could see that she wasn't thrilled, that something else was definitely bothering her. He was just about to question her more when Henry, their instructor, spoke up, "C'mon. It's time to get to work. I want us to finish the canvas tonight."


As Carolyn worked with her group on the final stages of the three-sided room they were creating, she couldn't help watching David. This time he was rolling out a blue sky with the same keen attention he'd given to painting the leaves.

He was driving her crazy. More and more he seemed to be insinuating himself into her life whether she wanted it or not and she had no idea why. Aside from kissing her silly when she nearly fell off the roof, the contact had been minimal—even today. And she didn't like to think of today's frolic in the water. It was altogether too intoxicating . . . too wonderful . . . too frightening.

When she wasn't thinking about him, she was worrying about her father. Twelve days until his surgery! No time to get used to the idea, no time to do all the things she'd ever wanted to do with him. Even now, the minutes seemed to be speeding by like a locomotive out of control. She shouldn't be spending her time thinking about David Reid. She should be concentrating on her dad.

Dan watched Carolyn out of the corner of his eye. She should have been sparkling with delight over the news of her father's surgery. She'd hoped for it long enough. Something was definitely wrong. He knew Carolyn too well not to notice. He couldn't help but observe that she glanced over at David Reid frequently or that several times he'd seen a sheen of tears in her eyes. A strong urge to protect her swept over him. David Reid had better not have done something to cause her pain.

Finally, unable to watch her so obviously in distress, he caught her attention. It was nearly time to stop anyway. Sauntering casually over to her, he said quietly, "Let's go. I need to talk to you. The others can tidy up."

The fact that she did exactly what he'd suggested alarmed him even more. Carolyn had a strong sense of responsibility. Normally, she would have insisted on staying and putting everything away. Explaining to the others that they had to leave early, he led Carolyn out of the school and away from the coffee shop across the street. "Let's go along to the dairy. I feel like an ice cream cone."

As they walked along the street, Dan told her about his day. He amused her with the story of old Mrs. Nesbit who tried to bring three cats into his clinic in one cage. By the time they'd reached the dairy, she was laughing.

Together they chose double-scoop cones and then headed to the park to sit at a picnic table. Trees filtered the light from the nearby streetlamps so that they were private yet able to see each other.

Their cones were as large as billowing clouds on a hot day before a storm, each scoop shifting and melting quickly in the warmth of the evening. Dan waited until Carolyn had crunched the crisp tail of the cone before asking, "What's bothering you, Carolyn? You haven't been yourself all evening."

He saw tears well up in her eyes and thought dire thoughts about David Reid. She swallowed and answered, "It's Dad's surgery. It's in only twelve days." She fingered her tears away from her face, then said, "There's so little time. We've had no warning." Then, her voice trembling, she blurted out, "I'm so afraid, Dan. What if he doesn't make it?"

Not knowing what else to do, Dan reached over and pulled her head into the comfort of his shoulder. He let her weep, rubbing her back, knowing that she would feel better. Finally, she straightened and he offered her some tissues.

As she snuffled into them and wiped her eyes, she said, "I'm sorry. I don't usually fall apart like this."

Trying to ease her distress, Dan teased, "I thought you must have had a major row with David Reid. You certainly watched him enough tonight."

He thought she would have gone off like a rocket as she had done every other time she'd discussed her employer. Instead she turned slightly away from him and examined the mess of tissue in her hands.

Finally she whispered, "I don't know what's happening to me, Dan. He's on my mind all the time. Even when I should be thinking about my dad." She sighed and shoved the tissues in her pocket. She struggled for words. "I'm so attracted to him. The chemistry is overwhelming. I've never felt like this before, not even with James."

Dan studied her with sympathy. He was just beginning to experience the same feelings every time he was near Cindy. "Would it be such a bad thing, being attracted to David?"

"He's not what I thought he was. At first, I thought he was just another version of James. But he's not. Usually, he's unaffected, thoughtful, and kind. Other times he's pigheaded and extremely aggravating. At the same time, he's quite endearing. He does everything with such gusto. Look at the way he painted that scenery, as if it was the most important thing in the world."

Dan smiled at that. He'd noticed how David always gave his best when he was interested, whether it was painting scenery or tennis. He supposed it was the ability to focus and concentrate that had made him the successful man he was.

"Is that bad?"

She shook her head wearily. "I don't know. I'm not sure I can handle a relationship right now." She looked at him and he could see the glimmer of tears again. "I'm not sure I could handle being hurt again."

I'd like to wring that James's neck, Dan thought. "Why would you expect to be hurt?"

She just sighed and muttered, "I don't know."

"What message is David sending to you? Is he acknowledging the attraction?" Dan knew the answer to that question. He'd seen David watching them, especially tonight when they'd left together. But he wanted to hear what she thought.

She blurted out, "He kissed me. He was so angry at me that he hauled off and kissed me blindly. And I was so mad, I kissed him back."

"And . . ."

She glanced at him under her lashes. "It was dynamite."

"What made him so mad?"

She shrugged her shoulders again and explained, "I tripped on the roof of his house and he thought I'd fallen off. I thought I was going to fall too, but Archie MacDougall caught me. I scared the wits out of all of us. David was furious with me and I blamed him for distracting me."

They sat silently, listening to the soft sound of the nearby river and the nighthawks calling overhead in the darkness. Out of the blue Carolyn added, "He's terrified of heights but today, he climbed a ladder and managed to reach the verandah roof. He said he did it because he wanted to be able to watch me on a roof instead of being frightened for my safety all the time."

Dan raised his eyebrows in the dark. So David really did care. Turning to him, she said quietly, "It was the bravest thing I've ever seen anyone do."

Dan reached out and took her hand where it lay on the table between them. "Caro. Why don't you just relax and let things happen. Enjoy the attraction. Give yourself a chance to see what develops."

David walked despondently down the street. By the time they'd finished the scenery and gone for coffee, Carolyn and Dan had disappeared. He'd been sure that they were just friends but now, he began to wonder.

Glancing over into the park, he saw them sitting in the gloom of a large maple. But there was still enough light from the streetlamps for him to see Dan reach out and take Carolyn's hand. Resisting the urge to go over and snatch her hand away from Dan, he found his truck and got in it. Starting it with trembling hands, he surged out onto the street and roared down the road toward home.

## *Chapter Nine*

Carolyn stood at the open window at David's house enjoying the early morning scene. The trees wore their lush summer greens, the grass was still sparkling with dew. Amid the sound of songbirds, the clear, pure sound of orioles calling back and forth reminded her of the spring day when she had first heard them with David.

It was thirty-six hours now since her father's announcement and she felt much more in control of her emotions. She could be with her father without tears flooding her eyes and accept that the surgery was the best of a bad situation.

She'd also gained some emotional distance when she thought of David. Her panic the other evening must have been the result of the strange sense of unity they'd shared in the lake. Whatever, she decided that dealing with her feelings for David had to wait until after her father's operation. For now, she'd try to keep as far away from him as possible. Noise coming in the window from the other side of the room reminded her that keeping such a resolution might be harder than she imagined.

Looking out over the verandah toward the cabin, she was amused to see David directing activities like a ringmaster in a circus tent. A strange skill for someone who couldn't choose a color or a kitchen cupboard door. The fact that he was stripped to the waist so early in the morning didn't help her resolve to ignore him.

Peter and David's nephew, Kevin, a boy of similar age, were busy putting up two screened eating tents. David's father and brother were moving topsoil with those tiny caterpillar tractors common to nurseries. His mother, sister Susie and sister-in-law were spreading the soil as were other helpers they had brought with them.

David also had her own family orchestrated into the action. Mike's truck was rumbling up the hill with another load of soil. Ben was busy running a water line from the house out to the tents and Andy was providing power. Even Cindy was in on the act. Her restaurant was providing food and services for both lunch and supper and, Carolyn understood that Dan had been invited. Was David playing cupid as well? she wondered.

The Nortons were removing the windows to prepare for the new ones coming on Monday while she had been stapling plastic over the openings. She'd fled upstairs because she wanted to escape David's enthusiastic praise for her work every time a member of his family passed by. As far as she was concerned, he was laying it on a bit too thick. His family were beginning to be just a little too interested in her.

She'd almost finished the windows when she heard people coming up the stairs. With a sinking heart, she recognized the voices of David and his mother. Who knew what he would be up to this time.

However, it was not quite as she expected. Nancy Reid, a tall, charming woman with greying hair and eyes like David's entered the room with David lagging behind, a very sheepish look on his face, as if he'd opened the barn door and all the horses were escaping. Putting down her tools and shoving her hands in her shorts' pockets, she waited to see what was up.

After hemming and hawing for a moment, he said, "Mom wants to know about the kitchen. I thought maybe you'd come downstairs and explain what's going on there."

Carolyn felt her mouth drop open. *What was going on there*? Why, nothing was going on there. Glancing at David, she saw that disarming look of absolute panic that he wore every time she mentioned the word "kitchen." Remembering her resolution to resist him and his problems, she ignored his unspoken plea for help. Anyway, irritating him a little would make up for the fact that he was driving her crazy.

She took his mother's arm and led her toward the doorway. "I'd be glad to explain what we've decided on," and added with a meaningful glance over her shoulder at David, "So far."

Leading them down to the kitchen, she began at the back door that led to the little verandah set in the angle of the two wings. "David and his family will enter through this door during bad weather."

Turning toward the framed-in room next to the entrance, she indicated the mudroom. "His children can leave their dirty clothes here if they've been romping out in the mud. All his wife will need to do is drop the clothes into the washing machine and the dryer. You can see we've got the wiring all ready for the appliances."

His mother was delighted. Turning to David, she said,

"Davie, how practical you've become. I always wanted such an arrangement but our house never lent itself to it."

Urging them on, Carolyn showed them the next room. "This room is to be David's wife's study or workroom. David wants it wired for every eventuality." Ignoring David's warning frown, she continued, "His wife can slip away from the kitchen to rattle off a few words on her word processor or sew a shirt for one of the children . . . or David."

David rolled his eyes.

By now, Carolyn was really enjoying herself. It was much more fun to tease him than to drool over him. She led them into the area intended for the kitchen and family room. The old cupboard, sink, and linoleum had been removed so that there was nothing there but an empty space with a new underfloor.

Just as David's mother asked, "What's happening here?" Ben wandered in. Before Carolyn could have the moment she'd been waiting for, before she could explain that David's wife was going to plan the kitchen, Ben piped up, "The kitchen is progressing and it's going to be fab-u-lous. You should see the models Carolyn made of it."

Ben's words hung in the air as both she and David gaped at him. David was the first to recover. His eyes absolutely gleamed with interest. He purred, "You've made models of the kitchen, Carolyn?"

Trying to stay calm and control the blush of embarrassment that threatened to give her away, she answered casually, "I was just fooling around. I do it all the time. Don't I Ben?"

But Ben wasn't listening. Instead he continued enthusiastically, "I could bring the models back when I go to pick up Dad for lunch. I'll bring the models of the house too. They're really neat."

Before Carolyn could get a word in edgewise, Nancy said enthusiastically, "I'd love to see the models, Carolyn. Maybe I'll get some ideas for our kitchen. It's time it was remodeled."

Accepting defeat, she turned to Ben. "Bring them over and you can set them up on the long verandah." Turning to Nancy, she explained, "If you'll excuse me now, I have to finish covering the window openings. We expect the new windows Monday morning and hope to start installing them immediately."

David watched as she walked to the door. He grinned and followed her. He just couldn't resist a little teasing. It would keep the sparkle in her eyes instead of the look of panic that occasionally lurked there.

As he followed her upstairs, he noted that Carolyn was definitely making a statement today. She wore new beige shorts topped with a bright green T-shirt. Her hair was tied back with a matching green ribbon and her flowered workboots were topped by green socks with a little frill along the top. A reminder to him, he figured, that she was nothing like the dreaded Linda.

He waited for a moment until she started to work, then sauntered in. "Well, Ms. Thompson, did you enjoy yourself down there? Hmmm? What exactly were you going to tell my mother?"

Giving him a bland look, she replied, "The truth, what else?"

"And that truth was?"

"Take your choice. Either that you hadn't a clue what you wanted or that you expected your wife to decide on a plan."

David grinned. "And why didn't you mention either of these, dear Carolyn?"

She blushed. "You know darn well why I didn't. I didn't get the chance."

"And why was that, Carolyn?"

She turned away from him and began to staple plastic with a vengeance. "Go away, David. Go play ringmaster outside."

Taking pity on her, he gave up annoying her and wandered out of the room, whistling an irritating tune.

Carolyn stopped her stapling and listened as his feet descended the stairs then turned and leaned against the wall. Her embarrassment down in the kitchen was going to be nothing compared to how she was going to feel when Ben brought in those models. Not only had she made them of the house and kitchen the way David and she had agreed. She'd also made models of the ground floor of the house and kitchen with the cabin restored to its original location.

The cabin was a large structure, large enough to contain a study at one end and two small rooms where it joined the kitchen. In these rooms she'd placed the wife's study and the mudroom. The washer and dryer she'd incorporated into the kitchen area. A passage led from the kitchen wing between these two small rooms to the study.

The kitchen and family area was the most innovative room she'd ever designed. Having the entire wing of the building at her disposal allowed her to make use of the light from the long windows on the two outside walls.

Instead of placing the actual kitchen area along the walls, she'd placed it in the center. The work area was hexagonal with entrances through each of the six angles. On some of the hexagonal's sides, she'd suspended cupboards from the ceiling thus allowing light to flood into the kitchen area. Wide counters provided great work space and ample storage.

In the section nearest the windows, she'd created an eating area with a large pine table. Because there was so much space, she'd created a reading nook in the corner with a window on either side.

On the other side of the kitchen proper, she had placed the family room with a fireplace, bookcases and media center. The result was a family living area that was light, airy and accessible in good weather through the door leading to the long verandah.

She was proud of her design. That wasn't what dismayed her. It was the fact that she designed the kitchen in direct opposition to what David wanted by using the cabin. It was a clear statement of disagreement with her client. She had never intended anyone should know about it, except the members of her family who were used to her experimenting.

Even worse, in making the model, she had definitely stepped into territory where she did not belong. David had said he wanted his wife to design the kitchen. What if he thought she was angling for that position? And of course, she wasn't.

Finishing the stapling of plastic on the last window, she hurried outside to find Ben. Drawing him to one side, she said, "Since you were so keen to bring in those models, Ben, I suggest you set them up well before lunch and invite people to see them before they eat."

Ben frowned. "Why do I get the idea I've just committed a major sin?"

"Let's just say, brother dear, that you're very lucky I love you so much or you just might wish you'd never been born. I was experimenting with ideas when I made two of those models. They were never intended for public viewing. However, since everyone knows about them now, you look after them."

With that, she hurried off to join Hugo and the teenage helpers, Ted and Philip. When she'd learned of David's family visit, she'd picked up the materials for the shed and with Hugo's help, had them transported down to the beach. By now, she expected to find they had finished the floor on which to frame the walls. She intended to make this a lesson for the boys and Hugo, who had never done this before.

Glancing at her watch, she saw that it was only 9:00. Ample time for them to get the small structure up and doors fitted so that it could be used for changing.

When Ben arrived with his father, David hurried over to lead Jim to a quiet area under the trees, where he could relax on a lounger and see everything as well. Then he returned to help Ben with the models. David couldn't help but notice that Ben was subdued as they carried the boxes over and placed them on a makeshift table made of boards placed on wooden workhorses. He wondered what was up.

Ben explained tersely, "I'd like everyone to have a look at these before lunch. Why don't you go and ask anyone interested to come over."

Although curious to see what was in the boxes, David did as he was instructed. It turned out everyone there wanted to see the models so David had to wait for a few minutes. Finally, he found himself looking at the model of the two floors of the house as they'd planned it and beside it, the kitchen he'd selected. She's incredible, he thought. She's worked everything out to scale. The only room she hadn't touched was the dining room.

Finally, he moved on to the next set of models. He already sensed that there was something special about them because Ben had placed them so they would be seen last and because everyone seemed to be excited about them.

As he approached them, a worried Ben stressed, "I don't think Carolyn ever intended anyone to see these. She says she was just experimenting with ideas."

Really interested now, he stepped up to the model of the house. Immediately, he saw that she'd moved the cabin back to the original location. For a few moments, he was really annoyed but when he looked closer, he saw that she'd made a study at the end of the structure. She'd even placed a large desk right at the end where it would have a view out of windows on three sides. The study was lined with shelves and there was a reading area before a fireplace. In a corner there was a tiny kitchenette.

The study was insulated from the rest of the house by the mudroom and the lady's study that was constructed in the space at the rear of the cabin.

He moved on to the kitchen. He could see she'd really spent a lot of time on this model. She'd even painted sunshine pouring in the windows over the eating area. The kitchen itself was suspended like a gem in the center. In the family room, she'd placed a tiny game of monopoly on the floor.

He loved it. He should have trusted her judgement from the start and listened to her. He had been too busy reacting to her great, thumping workboots to use his common sense.

Looking around, he realized that Carolyn was nowhere to be found. Returning to Ben, he asked, "Where's your sister?"

A worried Ben replied, "I think she's down at the beach."

David grinned and punched him lightly on the arm. "Relax. That's the most beautiful kitchen I've ever seen. The entire concept is outstanding."

He found her alone at the beach and, as usual, she was part way up a ladder pounding nails into a board forming part of the roof.

It didn't take a brain surgeon to determine that she was down here hiding. Her brother had put her on the spot. And David was glad he had. The models told him so much about her. He knew now that she loved the old house at least as much as he did, even though her vision was different. He also knew how extremely gifted she was and, if he wanted to win her, he would have to respect that gift just as his family had respected his.

Finally, taking his courage in his hands, he walked over and cautiously stood on the first rung of the ladder. As she felt the ladder shift under his weight, she peered down over her shoulder.

He reached up and gently placed his hands around her waist. "Come on down, madame architect."

At that, she spun around on the ladder, forcing him to step back on the ground. He held up his hand for her. "Come down," he coaxed again, "Let me tell you how brilliant your kitchen is."

She descended the ladder cautiously, never taking her eyes from him. Finally, she whispered, "Which kitchen?"

He thought of teasing but he could see that she was too anxious. "The one with the study in the old summer kitchen, which I might add, every man present was envious of."

By now, she was standing so close that he could see

tiny flecks of sawdust in her hair, sense her fragrance, feel the heat of her body reaching out to him.

"You're not mad?" she asked.

"No."

She still stood there, as if not sure what to do next. He couldn't resist reaching over and gently brushing her hair. He smiled. "You've got sawdust all over your hair."

She reached up and touched her hair. "I have?"

He wanted to kiss her but she had that fraught look, as if she'd had all she could take. Instead he took her hand. "Come. The food will be all gone if we don't get up there soon."

As they moved across the clearing toward the path, he paused, giving himself a tiny reward for his self control. "And thanks," he said, kissing her lightly on the corner of her mouth. "Thanks for getting the shed ready for the swimmers."


By 4:00 that afternoon, Carolyn was able to leave her work and come down to the beach. After a cooling swim she headed for the rock. Climbing up on it, she eased back on the warm granite, closed her eyes and breathed a sign of utter bliss. The sun still had enough strength to heat her body and relax her muscles.

For a while she dozed. Slowly she awoke to the sounds of people talking. Cindy, Dan, Barbara, and Ben were sprawled out on a blanket watching the two little girls play in the water. Close to shore David sat in the row boat with the two boys fishing. She smiled at that. He was having as much fun as they were.

She'd been surprised when the Reids had finished the landscaping early enough to enjoy the rest of the day. David's parents and sister had taken her father back to rest before they set out to wander through the stores in town. They would all return in time for a barbecue at 6:00.

One mystery had been solved. She'd been standing in line right behind David and his mother waiting to fill her paper plate at lunch when she heard Nancy ask, "How are you managing with all the ladders around, David?"

He turned and grinned at Carolyn. "Carolyn will tell you that I have made a fool of myself on several occasions. I wish I knew why heights and ladders bother me so badly."

Nancy looked surprised at this. "You don't remember? I always thought you knew."

"Remember what?"

"As an adventurous five year old, you were into everything. For awhile, you seemed to have no fear and we really worried about you. One day, your father left a ladder standing against the garage while he went to get something. I was in the house when I heard a clatter and then, the sound of you screaming."

Turning to Carolyn, she said, "I'll never forget it nor will his dad. There was David hanging by both hands from the eaves. The ladder was on the ground below. John made it around the corner of the garage in time to catch him just as he let go."

Carolyn looked at David with understanding. "No wonder the sight of me prancing along a ridgepole gave you a panic attack."

But David wasn't letting her get away with that. "No, my dear Carolyn, it was the sight of you falling off the ridgepole that scared me out of a year's growth."

Turning to his mother, he said, "You see the roof ridge of the kitchen section? She actually lost her footing and began to fall. I never did understand how she managed to stop the fall."

At his mother's horrified expression, Carolyn explained, "One of the roofers caught my arm and slowed me down so that I could get my footing on those slats you can see on the roof."

She was brought back to the present by water splashing across her legs. Sitting up, she found Ben laughing up at her. "Am I forgiven?"

"For splashing me?"

He grabbed her ankle and gave a tug. "No, Caro, for the models."

She pretended to consider. He yanked her down toward the water. "You've got thirty seconds."

Laughing, she managed to free her foot. "Okay, I forgive you."

Ben took another swipe at her leg. "And . . ."

"And what . . . ?"

"How about thanks."

He didn't have to explain. She knew what he meant. "Okay, thanks. My kitchen will look terrific in the house. So will the addition on the back."

Sending another spray of water in her direction, Ben turned and began to tease the two little girls.

Carolyn settled back down, stretching her arms above her head to get the full benefit of the sun. She felt a great sense of pride, knowing that David liked the new plan for the house. She hadn't realized how much she'd resented having to hide her ideas, hadn't realized how happy she would feel knowing that the house would be just right.

Suddenly, she was aware of Dan's voice and Cindy's squeal. Glancing over, she saw Dan chasing Cindy toward the water, a very determined gleam in his eye.

A surge of envy welled up inside her. David and she had never had time for fun like that. There had been no teasing, no flirting. Realizing what she had just thought, she groaned to herself. Where had that idea come from? She and David were not a couple. They'd spent very little time alone together. In actual fact, they spent most of their time aggravating each other.

Deciding she'd had enough sunbathing, she slid off the rock and went to the shed to change.


David leaned over and pulled an oar to turn the boat so he could see Carolyn sunbathing and then sprawled back against the bow, his fishing pole resting against the gunwale. Pulling his hat down over his eyes, he studied her unobserved.

He couldn't keep his eyes off her. It was bad enough to see Carolyn daily in jeans or shorts, let alone her little tennis skirts, but in a bathing suit? He shook his head wearily.

As he watched, she raised her arms to cover her eyes and he was transfixed. He closed his eyes and tried to think of putting worms on a hook, to distract his attention. If the boys hadn't been there, he would have banged his head against the bow of the boat in frustration.

He gave himself five minutes before he dared to peek at the rock again, only to discover that she had disappeared. Deciding the boys were old enough to be in the boat alone if the others stayed at the beach, he dived over the side and made for the beach. Grabbing a towel, he called to the others to watch the boys and headed for the shed.


Carolyn stood in the center of the empty kitchen space and thought about her model. The newly framed rooms at one end would have to be removed but that was no problem. In her imagination, it was Thanksgiving. A table sprang to mind with a centerpiece of gourds, fruit, and leaves. Yellow candles were ready to light and yellow table napkins marked each diner's place. She could imagine David sitting at one end with the members of his family as guests and at the other—at the other end . . . Carolyn closed her eyes. She couldn't bear it. She didn't want someone else sharing this dream.

She turned to concentrate on the area where the kitchen cabinets would be suspended over the ample counters. She could almost smell the turkey cooking in the eye-level oven. She could imagine the vegetables on the stove top ready for cooking and the cranberry sauce set in old-fashioned pressed glass dishes. Again, she fought against the notion that someone else would use this kitchen and serve this meal.

A sound made her turn and she was startled to discover David standing in the doorway watching her. She'd been so deeply in her daydream she hadn't even heard him.

He walked toward her with a look of intensity she'd never seen in his eyes before. "Are you imagining your kitchen?" he asked.

Embarrassed now, as if for some reason he could actually have read her mind and seen the holiday preparations, she turned away from him. "I've been trying to imagine how your wife would like this kitchen. I have to decide whether to go with neutral colors that would allow her to add her own touches or just take a chance and make a bold statement that might please."

He startled her by placing his hands on her shoulders and turning her around. Putting his finger under her chin, he raised her head and said, "Carolyn, I said I wanted my wife-to-be to choose the kitchen and I meant it. And I've asked you to design it."

She frowned. "But . . ."

With a wry smile, he watched her grapple with the logic of his statement. He was driven to distraction by her nearness. Along her hairline, tiny little curls had formed as her hair dried. Her face was flushed from the sun. Even after her swim, her fragrance reached out and surrounded him.

He couldn't resist teasing one of the little ringlets along the side of her forehead. She jumped at this but he persevered, drawing his finger down her jawline toward her lips. Then he spelled it out again, "Carolyn, I said I wanted my wife to design the kitchen. You are the one I want."

He knew very well that at one level she knew exactly what he was saying but was, for some reason, ignoring the truth. With a hiss of exasperation, he took her face in his hands, drawing his thumbs across her sweet lips. He felt her tremble. "Carolyn," he muttered, "I want you." And without giving her a chance to object, he tasted her satin lips until she gasped and opened to him.

At that she leaped away as though scalded, but only as far as his arms would allow. Part of him was amused because she had a grip on his shirt as if she was afraid he'd disappear.

Pulling her back against him, he held her there, caressing her nape and urging her head to his shoulder. "Carolyn. I love you," he said roughly. "I'm asking you to design the kitchen because I want you to be my wife. Can I make it any clearer?"

She still stayed in the shelter of his arms, her fingers clinging to his shirt. Finally, she lifted her head and looked at him with a troubled gaze. His heart sank. This was not what he wanted.

Slowly, she eased her fingers away from his shirt and

stepped away. She shook her head, trying to get her wits about her.

"Is the idea so repulsive?" he asked.

Her hand fluttered toward him, then fell by her side. She shook her head again and whispered, "David, I don't know. I don't trust myself where love is concerned. I thought I knew what love was before but it ended in heartbreak."

But David was not accepting this. He reached over and took her hand. "Look at me, Carolyn. I love you and I think you love me. We've been attracted since the first moment we saw each other."

She tried to pull away but he hauled her back until she stood with her hands against his shirt. "But I don't trust this attraction, David. I'm not good at judging what it means. It's probably just lust."

He stroked her throat and the sensitive place around her ear. "I know I feel more than lust. I feel love, love that I want to show you in every way. I want to share my life with you, to raise a family with you."

When she stood still, her eyes closed, trembling against him as he continued to caress her, he decided enough was enough.

Taking her hand, he led her to the door and out onto the verandah. The area between the cabin and the house was deserted. He pulled her down beside him on the verandah steps. When she tried to reclaim her hand, he held it. "Listen to me, Carolyn. I know this is a bad time for you. I know you need all your energies to deal with your father's operation. I can wait. I am sure I love you and I know you love me. Sooner or later you'll be able to accept that as the truth.

"And be warned right now. Whether you like it or not, I intend to care for you over the next difficult days. I have a condominium your family will use while in Toronto. I intend to be right by your side whenever you need me. I will not abandon you."

And then, to emphasize his point, he kissed her again, a long, searching kiss that left them both breathless.


David leaned against a tree and watched the scene. It was after 9:00 now on a perfect June evening when the glow of the sunset still brightened the western sky. Everyone except his parents, his sister and Jim Thompson were sitting around a crackling bonfire roasting marshmallows. They had moved into the cabin to play cards.

David leaned against the tree and watched. In many ways, it had been a great day. All the work was done and everyone seemed to have had a good time. And he had had to go and spoil it for himself and obviously, for Carolyn. She'd avoided him all through supper and only now sat down with the others.

David was just trying to decide whether he should join the group at the bonfire when a voice said, "I didn't expect to find you off by yourself."

Turning, he discovered his mother standing beside him. "I thought you were playing cards."

"We were but the men started talking so I thought I'd steal a few moments to be with you. It's the first time I've had all day. You kept us all so busy." She stood watching the scene for a moment, then said, "Are you happier now, David?"

"Much."

"The house is very beautiful. You must be proud of it. Carolyn and her family are quite a find."

He smiled wryly. "She's that all right."

She nodded her head knowingly. "I thought it was like that."

"Like what, Mother dear."

"Don't be obtuse, Davie. You know exactly what I mean."

David stood silently for a few moments. Finally, he said, "I told her I loved her today and asked her to marry me."

His mother raised her eyebrows at this news. "I gather you didn't get the reaction you wanted or you wouldn't be standing under the trees instead of joining the group."

"She said she wasn't sure what love was. That she wasn't sure what she felt. I told her exactly how I felt and that I intended to look after her over the next few days while her father has his surgery. I also told her she loved me. At that she fled."

He shrugged his shoulders. "So you see, with my usual determination to get my own way, I've probably botched my chances."

"I think you need to let Carolyn have space. She's got a lot on her mind right now. Give her a chance to test her feelings."

"So you think I have a chance?"

"Let's say I think she's very interested."

Voices called from the cabin. "Guess the others have discovered I was missing. Relax Davie. I'm sure it will all turn out okay. Follow your instincts."

David thought about this advice for a few moments and decided his mother was right. He would follow his instincts. And the only instinct he had now was to go down and join Carolyn by the fire.

Carolyn held the long stick bending under the weight of a marshmallow out over the flames. Just as she was about to pull it back, it burst into flames and, before her eyes, oozed off the end of the stick and fell sizzling into the fire.

A voice whispered in her ear, "That's not how you toast a marshmallow."

Carolyn groaned. How had David managed to get so close without her knowing it? Even as she wondered about this, he pushed his way in between Peter and her and sat down. Taking her stick, he whispered, close to her ear, "Here, let me roast you a marshmallow, my love." His breath caressed her neck and the hair on it stood up.

Carolyn glanced around hurriedly to see if anyone had heard that particular endearment but no one seemed to have taken notice.

He took the stick and in doing so, managed to settle himself closer to her, his left arm behind her, his right leaning forward with another marshmallow on the stick. She tried to close her mind to his nearness, to his scent. She watched with fascination as he twirled the stick above some embers. Even before he finished toasting the marshmallow golden brown, she knew what he was going to do.

When it was just right, he drew back the stick and, waiting a moment for the candy to cool, pulled it off and held it out for her to nibble from his fingers.

In the firelight, she could see that intensity in his eyes again as he dared her to accept his offering. When she hesitated he moved the mass of sticky sweetness just close enough that his fingers touched her lips. She gasped at the sensation and he thrust the sugary mess inside. As her lips closed over it, they touched his fingers again. Never taking his eyes off her, he licked his fingers.

Carolyn closed her eyes as she swallowed the sweet

mixture. He was trying to seduce her right in front of her family and friends. She tried to move away but he settled in more closely, then placed another marshmallow on the stick. Mesmerized, she watched him repeat the operation again and again, pulling off the sweet marshmallow and offering it to her, touching her lips as he let her nibble at it and finally, licking his fingers.

She forgot about the people around. She was only conscious of their own little space where she and David were bound in a tiny ritual of feeding, touching and tasting, and she was lost. Lost to the touch of her lips, lost to the warmth of his shoulder against her, lost to everything but his will.

Finally, there were no more marshmallows. He leaned over and with a finger, brushed away a dusting of white powder from her lips and she wished that he would kiss the sweetness off but the others were still there, listening to the strains of Andy's guitar. The sad notes touched her deeply. Sensing her mood, David pulled her against him and wrapped his arm around her, making her feel safe and desirable. For awhile, she gave into the luxury of believing this was love, but in her heart she was still unsure.

## *Chapter Ten*

**C**arolyn drove her van along the county road toward David's. It was ten days since her father's successful surgery and he had returned home the previous afternoon. They were all still floating on a high of happiness at their father's recovery. His cheeks were pink again, and even though he was recovering from a very intrusive surgery, he still had more energy than he'd had before.

She wondered now how they could have managed without David's kindness. The use of his condominium had allowed them to either walk or ride a streetcar over the short distance to the hospital. He had been there whenever she needed him, sitting with her during the interminable hours of the surgery, holding her when she wept with joy over its success, and insisting on driving her father and herself back to Stewart's Falls when he was released.

She had learned to depend on him, to need his presence and yet, she was not sure if that was enough. Being in love should be simple and straightforward. You should know how you feel, she thought. Then why am I still dithering?

She turned up the lane that led to the house but stopped a little way before she reached it. She wanted to enjoy looking at it, observing the fully installed windows and the beginning of the new roof the MacDougalls were busy working on. The presence of Andy's truck suggested that he was hard at work completing the wiring. A large van told her that the men hired to install the heating and cooling system were also hard at work.

Walking around the house to the kitchen verandah, she was surprised to see a ladder, and even more startled to discover David on the fifth rung. One white-knuckled hand gripped the ladder while the other hand sanded the old paint on the verandah eave.

It was at that moment that she knew. That crazy act of bravery and stubbornness won her heart more than any other thing he had ever done.

For awhile, she just stood there, watching, admiring the beauty of his movements, the length of his bare legs and the play of muscle as he reached and scraped. Finally, she could stand it no more. Unable to resist the urge, she stepped up to the ladder and carefully took hold of his ankle.

As he stiffened at her touch, she said clearly, "David Reid. I love you."

At the sound of her voice, he dropped the sanding block and literally slid down the ladder.

He turned, pulling the red kerchief he had tied around his head off and wiping the perspiration from his face.

She was touched by his look of uncertainty as he asked, "What did you say?"

She walked toward him and reached up, cupped his

face with her hands and said, "I love you, David Reid. Will you marry me?"

"Oh, Carolyn," was all he could say before he hauled her into his arms and kissed her. Winding her arms around his neck she returned his kisses, murmuring how sorry she was that it had taken her so long to accept.

They finally came up for air in time to hear Angus MacDougall say from above, "Well, Archie, I see wee Carolyn has got her man."

# Epilogue

On a day in October when the trees flamed against the autumn blue of the sky, David stood at the front of the church waiting for the sight of his beloved. The wedding music started and everyone stood up.

At first, all he could see were the nieces and nephews coming up the aisle; the little girls walking beside the boys, wearing golden velvet dresses and carrying bouquets of burgundy chrysanthemums.

And then she was there, his lady with her proud father, dressed in a long slim ivory gown embossed with seed pearls around the neck and cuffs of the long sleeves. A band of ivory set across her brow suspended a veil at the back.

As she approached, he could see her hair was seeded with pearls and seemed to disappear into a long seeded braid behind her shoulders. How had she known that he saw her as his chatelaine, the lady of his heart and home?

Just before she moved beside him, she paused and

lifted one side of her skirt just enough to show him that she was shod in white workboots encrusted with pearls. Smiling demurely and dropping her skirt, she moved beside him.

David took her hand when her father gave her away and never taking his eyes away from hers, he lifted it to his lips. For a moment they stood, suspended in time, making their own silent vows. The harrumph of the minister brought them back to the present.

They exchanged their vows, never taking their eyes off each other. When the minister asked David, "Do you take this woman to be your lawfully wedded wife?" he stated clearly, "I do," and whispered so only his bride could hear, "Workboots and all."